THE BLOODSTAINED CROSSING

In the town of Rawton, a man's death coincides with John Probity's arrival. By the next day another person has died and Probity is in jail, accused of murder. Freed by the enigmatic town barber, Ulysses Court, Probity sets out to discover the truth. With the number of dead rising, Probity and Court witness the gunning-down of some Mexicans at the San Pedro River. Can they make their way to safety and stay one step ahead of the gun-toting outlaws?

OLDHAM

MATT LAIDLAW

THE BLOODSTAINED CROSSING

Complete and Unabridged

LINFORD
Leicester

First published in Great Britain in 2012 by
Robert Hale Limited
London

First Linford Edition
published 2014
by arrangement with
Robert Hale Limited
London

A catalogue record for this book is available
from the British Library.

ISBN 978–1–4448–1924–3

Published by
F. A. Thorpe (Publishing)
Anstey, Leicestershire

Set by Words & Graphics Ltd.
Anstey, Leicestershire
Printed and bound in Great Britain by
T. J. International Ltd., Padstow, Cornwall

This book is printed on acid-free paper

PART ONE

Prologue

June 1881

It was the distant creaking of timber that dragged her out of a deep sleep. When she turned over in bed and sat up, yawning, the jingle of harness and the squeal of dry wheel boxes told her that a wagon was being driven down the overgrown trail that passed within fifty yards of the house. It sounded heavy. She knew instinctively that it must have come from one of the silver mines located around Tombstone, but she couldn't understand why, or what it was doing on that disused trail.

Then, as her searching hand touched nothing but a warm sheet on the other side of the bed, she realized that she was alone. At the same time she caught the clear sharp scent of the night air. The front door was open. Ralf, a light

3

sleeper, had woken before her and was outside in the front yard.

Swiftly she slid out of her bed. The hard floor was cool under her bare feet. She shivered, slipped on a light robe over her thin nightgown, then left the bedroom and walked quickly across the living room with its dark furniture. There was a high moon. Its pale light flooded in through the open door. Ralf's elongated shadow lay across the floor. She stepped through it, felt a sudden chill, touched his shoulder and pressed against his warmth.

He was standing side-on in the doorway, the moonlight touching his lean face as he gazed south towards the border. It ran east to west, an invisible line drawn between Arizona Territory and Mexico, and was just half-a-mile away down an easy gradient where tall saguaros reached for the clear skies. The old Springfield rifle was held loosely across his body. She nudged the butt with her thigh as she moved in close. He started, glanced at her. She knew he was absorbed in what he was doing, and she'd startled him. His eyes were dark.

'What?' she said.

'I don't know.'

'Wagons like that one,' she said, 'come from the silver mines. But midnight has long gone, that trail's never used. It wends its way down the slope for a few hundred yards, then peters out in the scrub. It goes nowhere.'

'It goes to the border,' he said.

'And?'

'I heard riders, that's what woke me up. There were horsemen outside when I came down, rough men, heavily armed, wearing sombreros with silver conchos glittering in the moonlight. They came riding up the trail, stopped short of the house, seemed to be looking into the distance. They were watching and waiting. Then I heard the wagon rumbling. Someone cursed gruffly as the wheels hit the dry ruts. Another man told him to shut up. The

Mexicans pointed, waved. I heard them laughing excitedly as they swung their horses and rode back down the slope.'

'So what does it mean?'

'You've seen the wagon. You know where it's from, so it's not too hard to work out what it's carrying. And it followed those Mexicans down to the border.'

He handed the rifle to her, and she saw that he had his battered pair of field glasses. He took a single step out of the doorway and lifted them to his eyes.

'Too dark, even with the moon,' he said. 'Can't see much. Shapes. Shadows. But they're unloading crates.'

'Mexicans can't carry heavy crates on horses — not even pack mules could do that.'

'Oh yes, they could. These are heavy, that's obvious from the way the men are moving, but they are not big. And there are not many of them. I think I saw three, no more. But their number doesn't matter, because there's no need to tie them onto mules. There's another wagon there. Under the trees, on the Mexican side of the border.'

She reached out, squeezed his arm, felt the tense muscles as he lowered the glasses and stepped back into the house.

'It seems obvious,' she said after a moment's thought, 'but if we're right about what's happening down there, a load of silver being . . . transferred like that — well, isn't that kind of thing illegal?'

'It is. And if that is what they're doing,' he said, 'then we could be in deep trouble.'

'Us?' She gripped both his arms fiercely, turned him so that he was facing her. 'I don't understand. Why should we be in trouble?'

'Because I was at the door when the wagon drove by,' Ralf said tonelessly. 'I was caught in clear moonlight, should have stepped back into the shadows but I was too slow. The man riding shotgun saw me. He took a good, long look, then deliberately lifted the shotgun high so I could see it and pointed in my direction. I could see his teeth. He was grinning. And he won't forget.'

1

One month later

John Probity was a tall man, strong and lean. He moved through life with grace and the balance of a dancer, could use knife or gun with bewildering speed and deadly accuracy, and was guided by a philosophy picked up from a ragged mountain trapper called Maxwell Golightly. That unique character had once told him that a battle could be lost for the want of a nail. A wise old-timer, wetly sucking on a blackened corn-cob as the light from the crackling camp-fire flickered across his bearded face, he had laboured on at some length.

Probity, a young man of eighteen at the time, had listened with impatience, understanding the story's logic but not its relevance to his own circumstances.

'Son, it's like this,' the old man had explained, amusement lurking in sharp eyes, almost buried beneath brows like curls of wool stripped from an old ewe. 'Ain't nothing stoppin' a young feller runnin' out the house without puttin' on his britches, but common sense should soon tell him that walkin' into town near as dammit buck naked, he ain't going to get very far.'

Never one to waste ammunition of any kind, Probity had grasped the idea, shaped it to his needs and consigned it to his subconscious for future use: *In life, if you're determined never to be caught with your pants down, think, then act; didn't matter who you were, it paid to spend vital seconds weighing up situations so that the next step you took didn't turn out to be your last.*

John Probity had lived by that philosophy for twenty years. That night, twenty-one years after he'd ridden away from a flickering camp-fire, the wise words spoken by a trapper called

Maxwell Golightly came howling back to haunt him.

★   ★   ★

Probity stepped out of the Starlight saloon a little unsteadily, and squinted across the street at the rooming-house. Although he hadn't seen her since noon, the plan was that Annie would ride into town and go straight up to the room. If she'd done that she would have waited with growing impatience for him to join her, and he felt an instant pang of guilt when he looked up at the first floor window. The light was out. He'd kept his foot planted on the brass rail fronting the bar for too damn long, and she'd gone to bed.

Yet he also knew he was being too hard on himself, perhaps on both of them. She'd gone to bed, not out of exasperation, but because she was worn out. He had entered the saloon with a purpose: Annie was desperate for information, and his aim was to probe

11

for it without revealing his intentions. So the conversations he started had been meandering in their nature, and became more so as the evening wore on and the men he spoke to sank yet more strong liquor.

In the end, Probity admitted, he had got nothing for his pains, and it was with some frustration that he peered down at the squashed shape of his unlit cigarette. He stepped away from the saloon, walking without watching where he was going, acting without thinking — but so what? It was late, there was but the one horse at the hitch rail — his roan — and the oil lamps were casting their warm glow over a dusty, deserted main street.

With the philosophy that had ensured his survival a long way from his mind and a lucifer proving difficult to grasp in the tight pocket of his vest, Probity poked blindly with two fingers as he took yet another step forward. Beneath his boot, dry wood splintered. Suddenly he was down on one knee. He toppled sideways, winced as his head cracked against the mesquite upright supporting the *ramada*. His Stetson slipped over his ear. He swore softly. Then, one leg dangling through a hole in the ancient plank-walk and the other doubled up beneath him, he began to laugh.

He was still laughing when he heard the unmistakeable sound of a six-gun being cocked. A ring of hard, cold steel was rammed into the back of his neck. Then, in front of him, a man seemed to step up out of a hole in the ground.

He'd been in the street, off to one side. Waiting. Probity hadn't seen him. Now he'd stepped up onto the plank-walk. Probity squinted up at him. He was a tall, lean man with a stony, unshaven face from which black eyes stared coldly. The face was made to appear darker and more menacing by his sand-coloured Stetson. A badge glinted on his vest. Unexpectedly, he grinned. His teeth flashed startlingly white. Then his six-gun caught the lamplight as, without warning, he swung it up out of the shadows. It struck Probity a vicious blow across the temple. Behind his eyes, red light flared. Consciousness slipped away like water out of a holed bucket, bringing with it an encroaching darkness. And all Probity could hear as he sank into a black, bottomless pit was a long-dead fire crackling and the faint echoes of an old trapper's laughter.

★　★　★

'You're in trouble,' said the man with the badge. 'You drifted into Rawton sometime yesterday, a big feller astride a big roan horse, a man who thinks he's as tough as old boots — but now you've gone too damn far.'

'You're talking nonsense. I'm no drifter. I have a reason for being here.'

'You think we care why you came? All we care about is the crimes you've committed in the past twenty-four hours.'

Probity's head was banging. The side

of his face was stiff with drying blood. He was slumped in a hard wooden chair. The room seemed overcrowded, airless. It was a small office, a square room fronting the town jail. Smoke hung in it like river mist. Three big men were watching him. Their very size made them threatening. Their presence, and the weapons they carried, radiated power.

The unshaven man with the badge had delivered his statement, a statement Probity was at a loss to understand. Now the deputy swung away. He struck a match and lit a cigarette; looked across at the man sitting behind the desk. The town marshal. The man, Probity figured, who had held a six-gun against the back of his neck while his deputy did his best to crack Probity's skull.

A third man was standing near the door. He was another big man, but where the lawmen carried muscle, this man was running to fat. The pistol he wore on a sagging belt was not a workmanlike tool, but a fancy weapon carried for show. He wore a dark suit, white shirt, black string tie, gold-rimmed spectacles. A cigar smouldered between thick fingers. Sweat glistened in his thinning grey hair.

'Crimes?' Probity said. 'I've had some interesting conversations, eaten well at the cafe, taken a drink in your fine saloon. D'you mind telling me which one of those is a crime?'

'Before I answer that,' said the man behind the desk, 'let's make this official. I'm Orin Craig, Rawton town marshal. That makes your arrest legal. You've had the pleasure of meeting my deputy, Gord Sager. As for crimes, what happened in the street you brought on yourself: you violently resisted arrest when leaving the Starlight saloon.'

The man by the door cleared his throat.

'My name is Ellis Quaig,' he said. 'I'm a witness to what happened up the street, and I also have certain information. Right now, I hold your life in my hands.'

Probity stared. 'My *life?* What the hell are you talking about?' He looked at Craig. 'All right, now you've made it official let's look at the facts. The first is clear: I did not resist arrest, violently or otherwise. The second is the one I'm waiting to hear from you: what was I being arrested for? What the hell am I supposed to have done?'

'You were falling-down drunk when you staggered out of the Starlight saloon — '

'Drunk?' Probity cut in. He shook his aching head, barked a laugh. 'The whole evening, I'd downed a couple of glasses of weak beer. You saying that pompous ass by the door is holding my life in his hands because you told him I was *drunk?*'

'When you rode into town last night, you accosted a young woman, went on to get too familiar with her,' Craig said. His voice was expressionless, his grey eyes cold. 'Seems you came to Rawton looking for her. You grabbed ahold of her when she came out of the store, did what looked like some heated talking. Come the hours of darkness, you had dinner together in Buck's diner — steak, eggs, apple pie, coffee, the whole works. Then with a grin on your face like a cat who's knocked over a jug of cream, you booked one room in Amy Bell's rooming house and you and that young lady spent the night there.'

Probity narrowed his eyes. 'So?'

'Together.'

'Yes.'

'A widow woman. She has her own house, down by the border.'

'I know that, it's why she shops here rather than Tombstone. But it was late, we had talking to do, she was tired and wasn't looking forward to the ride. Booking a room for the night made good sense.'

'You think so? I wonder where you went to church, where you learned morals, decent behaviour, the right way to treat a respectable lady.'

'Oh for God's sake,' Probity said. 'This is Rawton not Salt Lake City,

Arizona Territory not Utah, and sure as hell I'm no Latter Day Saint. But all that's beside the point. In this case, morals don't come into it.'

Craig didn't look unimpressed. Probity wasn't even sure if the man was listening, and the pain in his head became almost too much to bear when he was hit by a sudden, stone-cold certainty.

Christ, these men had no intention of letting him go. For some reason they had hunted him down, in the dead of night when there were no witnesses, and now . . .

'This morning,' Craig said, 'after spending the night alone in the room with that young widow, you rode out of town with her. Where did you go?'

'None of your damn business.'

'Did you head north, take the Apache trail snakes up through the hills?'

'I don't know. Took no notice. We rode out of town because we still had talking to do.'

'And now the talking's all done with,'

Ellis Quaig said from his position by the door. He'd removed the cigar from his lips. His face was split by a thin smile that got nowhere near his cold grey eyes. 'But you know that, don't you? You must know, because that's why you're here. There's the shadow of a rope hanging over your head, and — '

'No,' Probity said, a sudden hollowness in his belly. 'I don't know why I'm here, because the best you've come up with is a charge of drunkenness and that's good for maybe one night in a cell.'

'The widow is dead,' Sager said. 'The charge is murder, the penalty is death.'

John Probity rocked in the chair. It was as if a second blow from Gord Sager's six-gun had struck him, this time across the face, and again it was the deputy doing the delivering. There was the salt taste of blood in Probity's mouth and, as he stared at the big deputy in numb disbelief, he knew that when the shock hit him he'd bitten his tongue.

'Dead?' he said, the word slipping so faintly from his lips that it was as if all his strength had drained away.

'Ten mile from here,' Orin Craig said. 'Workers were taking a break. They were smoking in the shade of some disused sheds close to the Owl Creek silver mine in the Dragoon Mountains' foothills. Late afternoon. One of them noticed something. Sun was shinin' through what was left of the roof. Hittin' on something pale. They investigated, found her body. Annie Schäfer. Stripped naked. Throat cut.' He paused, let the silence build until it seemed to quiver with tension. 'But I'm telling you what you already know,' he said at last. 'You murdered Annie Schäfer, left her naked body tossed like a ragdoll among heavy pit props stacked at the back of a shed.'

Probity shook his head. His face was pale. 'She never left my side until we turned back. Then she headed for home, and we arranged to meet here. We were never, at any time, anywhere near Tombstone or the Dragoon Mountains. Hell, how far d'you think we'd ride for some private talking?'

'You rode out of Rawton with Annie Schäfer, rode back alone. The next time she was seen . . . ' Craig shook his head, his expression ugly. 'The next time she was seen she was dead, and before she died she'd been brutally raped.'

'Raped?' Probity squeezed his eyes shut, opened them again. 'If she was raped, that sure as hell should tell you I'm not your man.'

'There's no doubt. You did it, you'll hang.'

'Let me walk out of here, and I'll find somebody, somewhere, who can prove I'm telling the truth.'

'The next time you walk out of here,' Craig said, 'there'll be a rope and a gallows out back, a man with a prayer book, another with a blindfold.'

'I didn't kill her.'

'There'll be no need to waste a jury's precious time considering a verdict,' Ellis Quaig said in a matter of fact way, 'because you'll be lucky to see the inside of a court room, lucky to see this night out.'

'You talking about a lynching? For that to happen, word has to get out. So who's doing the talking, spelling it out? How does it go? Woman brutally raped, murdered, killer held in jail? Is that it? Who's going to be out there shooting his mouth off? You? These two upright, honourable lawmen?'

'Maybe the word's already out,' Quaig said.

'Yeah, and lawmen are duty bound to ensure the safety of prisoners, turn away lynch mobs.' Probity bit his lip, took a deep breath. 'D'you want to know why?'

'Why you killed her?'

'Why we were in that room together. Why it was not immoral, why I could no more have raped and killed her than . . . than . . . ' He stopped, blinking away tears. 'Her name was Annie Schäfer,' he said huskily, 'but you know that, that's about the one thing you've got right. But you also know she was a widow, so that was the name she took when she married. She kept it when her husband was murdered, shot by a drunk across the street from the Oriental Saloon — yeah, that's right, in Tombstone.' Probity's laugh was brittle. 'I'm here because she wanted me with her, and Rawton was the best place to meet. She was in some kind of trouble, or there was trouble brewing that she'd got wind of — both, more like it — and so she did what she always did at such times.'

Probity paused, looked at the watching men.

'She did what she'd done since she was a little kid,' he said softly. 'She sent for her big brother.'

He waited, listened to the soft sound of men breathing, the creak of a chair as Craig shifted his weight; caught the strong stink of his own stale sweat, the reek of Ellis Quaig's cigar, the coppery scent of his own blood that set nerves screaming.

'But you knew that too, didn't you?' Probity said when nobody bothered to break the silence. 'You knew Annie Schäfer was my sister, you knew she'd sent for me, and I'm here now because she's safely out of your way. Because you're playing some goddamn evil game, and you couldn't afford to have a nosy stranger running around loose.'

Orin Craig swung both boots up onto the desk and spat sideways into a basket.

'When you've finished exercising your jaws,' he said, 'my deputy'll take you out back and show you to your room.'

Probity met Craig's hard gaze, and forced a thin, mocking grin.

'Trouble is,' he said, 'the talking I did also included a lot of listening, and neither the listening nor the talking was all with Annie Schäfer. You weren't watching me close enough, fellers. I heard enough and passed on enough to cause you a heap of trouble, and putting me in an early grave won't stop all of your fine plans from falling down around your ears.'

2

They locked him in one of the four strap-steel cells in the bare premises behind the office. It was a small annexe built of solid stone blocks. In each cell the windows were rectangular slots punched high up in the walls, too small by far to let a man through, even supposing he could reach them and somehow rip out the iron bars.

The cell door clanged shut. Keys rattled in the lock, then jingled musically as Gord Sager sashayed out with the mincing gait of a painted dance-hall tart. The deliberate mockery showed that the deputy was in high spirits. Maybe he liked cracking men's skulls, was looking forward eagerly to watching Probity strung up by the neck. The solid wooden door slammed behind him, and he must have said something amusing as he returned to the office for there was a muffled burst of laughter.

Probity dropped heavily onto the corn husk mattress on the iron cot. He sat there, still dazed, still in pain, leaning forward with his elbows on his knees and hands hanging limp as he stared blindly at the dirt floor.

He had been close to shedding tears when they hit him with the news of Annie's death. Already weakened by the blow to the head, his vision blurred by pain, he'd come close to breaking down. But even before that shocking news he had been confused, unable to understand what was happening. And his bold parting words, blurted impulsively, had been pure bluff; he had talked to nobody since his arrival in Rawton, and knew nothing — certainly nothing that posed a threat to the two lawmen and Ellis Quaig.

The talks with Annie had starkly laid bare her fears, and the reason for them. She and her husband had one night watched a wagon drive down to the border. Heavy crates had been unloaded, and manhandled into Mexico. Ralf Schäfer knew that the man riding shotgun on the wagon had seen him watching but, when nothing happened, the incident had been half-forgotten. Then, outside Tombstone's Golden Eagle Brewery, Ralf Schäfer had been shot dead by a drunk wildly waving a dragoon pistol. That tragedy left Annie grief-stricken, but also frightened and bewildered. Coming as it did so soon after what they had witnessed at the border, she was convinced the killing had been a put-up job.

Fearful that she would be the next to die, she had got word to Probity. Knowing her story was too thin for him to get his teeth into, Annie had suggested that he should to talk to a man called Ulysses Court. She admitted she was clutching at straws. Court was filling the role of town barber — he'd taken the job when the incumbent had died suddenly from apoplexy — but his real reason for being in Rawton was shrouded in mystery.

Ralf Schäfer had his own opinions on

that mystery, and had approached Court quite soon after the border incident. Court had listened to his story while cutting the young man's hair. From his intense interest, and the length of time it took him to wield the scissors, Schäfer had his suspicions confirmed: he was convinced that the man was no barber. He'd questioned him in a roundabout way, but Court had simply told him with a grin that when sitting in a barber's chair most men couldn't stop talking. Taking the job, he said, was an excellent way of picking up all of a town's gossip without even trying.

But why, Ralf had wondered, would a man take on a job for which he was not fitted just to spend hours listening to garrulous old-timers?

Because of the air of mystery surrounding Court, Probity had taken Annie's advice seriously. He'd decided that the best way to approach him was to emulate Ralf Schäfer, drop in for a haircut or a shave, and start a casual conversation that would only get to the point if they were alone in the shop. But that had been planned for another day and, as Ellis Quaig had savagely pointed out, Probity would be lucky to survive the night.

And yet . . .

For all the lawmen's hard words and Quaig's glowering threat of imminent violence, the town remained quiet. Probity figured the window in his cell — too high to see out of — looked down on a rubbish-littered alley that sloped a short way to the main street, and if crowds had been gathering he would surely have heard the growing clamour, the cries of those exhorting the mob to action. But the only faint sounds that reached his ears came from the office: he listened to the clink of tin cups, the murmur of conversation, and then after a while all that changed when footsteps stamped across the room and the street door banged. Two people had walked out. Ellis Quaig, Probity guessed, was some sort of posturing town official, probably a leading light in the town council who figured he should be governing the territory. He would be heading home. It was highly likely that it was Marshal Orin Craig who had walked out at the same time, leaving Gord Sager on night shift.

It was also possible, as Probity had pointed out in his scornful accusation, that the marshal intended to broadcast the news that Annie Schäfer had been brutally done to death and that her crazed killer was locked up in the town jail. But was it *likely?* Probity thought not. It was late, well past midnight, and most people were in bed. Craig could hardly go knocking on doors, flashing his badge, and expect bleary-eyed men roused from deep sleep to answer his clarion call and form a raging lynch mob howling for Probity's blood.

No, the talk in the office had been carefully calculated to put the fear of God into Probity. He had been snatched off the street, and the three big men who had crowded him in the claustrophobic office and accused him of murdering his own sister wanted him to spend a sleepless night. They wanted him rigid and sweating on the thin mattress, staring wide-eyed into the darkness, jumping at shadows and in fear of his life; they wanted him softened up for whatever it was they had planned for him on the morrow.

Probity's hope was that they'd make sure crowds had gathered, then do nothing more than publicly ride him out of town on a rail. The other possibility, which he kept pushing to the back of his mind, was that a kangaroo court would assemble and he'd be convicted and hanged.

Two questions remained.

In the dead of night, Annie and Ralf Schäfer had witnessed an incident involving a wagon from one of Tombstone's silver mines and a bunch of armed Mexicans, and for that they had died. Probity knew now that his arrival in Rawton had sealed Annie's fate and, furthermore, the night's events proved that because they had been seen together his own life was in danger.

The first question was, what was so all fired important about the incident the Schäfers had witnessed?

The second question was, how the hell was Probity going to find the answer to the first question if he was locked in a cell with nothing to look forward to but the hangman's noose?

* * *

He must have fallen asleep, on top of the thin blanket.

It was cold, the chill mist of an Arizona night seeping in through the open barred windows. But what had awoken him was not the dampness that was like a wet cloth on his aching forehead but the sound of talking in the office. The voices were not raised, but there was an urgency, an intensity in the tone, that had reached him even in his unconscious state and put him immediately on the alert.

And now one man had begun to shout. There was an answer, much quieter, then the first man again, snapping back. Probity recognized Gord Sager's voice. The deputy managed to roar something that sounded like, 'Get the hell out — ' and then there was a dull thud and he stopped abruptly. For a few moments there was silence. Then the door was pushed open and Sager stumbled through, bareheaded, keys jingling in one hand, the other held to a wound on his face from which blood was trickling.

He had been helped on his way by a push from a man of medium height, wearing clothing that was mostly dark grey. The man's blue eyes seemed to blaze in a deeply tanned face. His flat crowned black hat was tilted at a jaunty angle, and the slight twist to the lips beneath a drooping moustache suggested constant amusement. He held a six-gun casually in one hand, and Probity guessed he had used it as a club to silence the big deputy. A dose of his own medicine. Probity found himself smiling, the movement of the muscles reminding him that his own face was still a mask of dried blood.

'Open the cell door.'

Still with a hand to his bleeding face, his eyes black with smouldering rage, Sager turned the key in the lock. The door swung open. Once again the grey-clad man pushed the deputy with a stiff arm that this time propelled him into the cell.

'Take your badge off. Give it to Probity.'

Knows my name, Probity thought. I don't know his. Or perhaps I do. This has to be Ulysses Court. I couldn't get to him, so he's come to me. And Ralf Schäfer was right. This man is no barber.

'You won't get away with this, Court,' Sager said, confirming Probity's suspicions.

'Are you going to stop me?' Court said, and as Sager handed his badge to Probity he said, 'I'm sorry about this, but I've got no choice,' and he whacked the deputy over the head with his six-gun.

There was a sickening crack that made Probity wince. Sager grunted. His eyes rolled, showing the whites, and he went down like a sack of grain.

Probity held up the badge. 'What's this for?'

'Pin it to your vest.'

'Who's that going to fool? You think a badge makes me invisible?'

'You've been in town just a couple of days. Sager's fancy Stetson's in the office. You're about his height and build. You walk out of here wearing his hat pulled well down and we stay in the shadows, nobody's going to take a second look. If anyone's around this late we keep walking, look as if we're deep in conversation. They'll see Deputy Gord Sager taking a walk with the town barber, maybe briefly wonder what's going on, then lose interest.'

Probity nodded, realizing that Court had thought this through and liking what he'd heard.

'I left my horse outside the saloon.'

'Mine's now tied next to yours, so we don't waste any time.'

'We make it that far, then what? Where are we going?'

Court gave him a level look from blue eyes showing a hint of compassion that was a dead giveaway.

'What's your best guess, in the circumstances?'

Probity nodded understanding. 'Annie's house.'

'Right.'

'That could be risky. After this, I'm a killer on the run. If they raise a posse, won't that be the first place they'll look?'

'You been there?'

'No. And all Annie told me was that it's about twelve miles south-east of Rawton.'

'That's true. It's within spitting distance of the border.' Court grinned. 'You see a posse coming over the hill, half-a-dozen long strides and you're in Mexico. Untouchable.'

'But that's not the plan.'

'You hightailing to Mexico? Oh no. But if we stand here discussing plans, that feller's likely to wake up and raise the roof before we get halfway up the street.'

'Then let's move.'

Probity was pinning Sager's badge to his vest as they walked quickly through to the office. He picked Sager's hat off the desk, slipped it on, tugged it down. His gun belt was hanging on a peg. He swept it down without stopping, was buckling it around his waist as he stepped through the open door and onto the plank walk.

A mangy dog saw him and ran across the street, its tail between its legs. Somewhere in an alley a cat wailed, but of human life there was no sign.

Behind him, Ulysses Court said, 'You smell anything?'

'Cigar smoke. Quaig was smoking one.'

'That was a while ago,' Court said thoughtfully. He looked left and right, said, 'Come on,' and started up the street.

3

Half a block down from the saloon, Orin Craig was in the deep shadows under the *ramada* sagging over the front of Jameson's Animal Feed store. He was leaning against the wall, talking to Ellis Quaig. The florid businessman held a fat cigar in his hand, and he was frowning as he looked down at the glowing tip.

'Getting John Probity locked in a cell is half the job done,' Quaig said. 'By dawn, I want him out of our hair for good.'

'I'm not sure I like what you're suggesting. You sure it's necessary?'

'If Probity is on the loose, he'll start digging. It's possible he's already heard too much, and now his sister's dead. John Behan's still hanging on as sheriff of Cochise County. If Probity got to him, Behan would be happy to tell him where his sister died. Christ only knows who murdered her, or why, but it's something we could have done without; her death leads Probity directly to Ronan Casey's Owl Creek mine. If he got that far it would still leave him a mile away from the truth, but in my opinion even that's too close for comfort.'

'You've got him in jail now — '

'And before morning, he'll be dead. Tell me I'm right, tell me I can trust you to make that happen.'

Craig shifted his weight uneasily. 'I've followed your orders so far, but what I'm doing for you is threatening my job. Behan may be an unpopular sheriff, but in Cochise County he's the man I answer to, and he's no fool. Getting rid of John Probity is a big risk, and I don't understand the urgency. What makes him such a threat?'

'Two things,' Quaig said. 'He worked as an assistant town marshal up in Dodge City, Kansas, got friendly with Wyatt Earp. Earp's been in Tombstone since '79. He was deputy under Behan, but couldn't get on with the man. Now he's a deputy US Marshal, and that means Probity has a dangerous friend.'

'And the second?'

'If Probity gets the chance, he'll go talking to Ulysses Court, and I've had my suspicions about that man ever since he rode into town. He has a man captive when he's all lathered up in his chair, asks too many probing questions, does a lot of listening. We never did discover what he got from his talk with Ralf Schäfer, which is one of the reasons we made a move.'

'Yeah, but surely you're worrying without cause. The way I see it it'd be mighty unusual if the town barber wasn't of a garrulous nature.'

'Ever thought that might be an image he's working hard to create? I've always feared word of what's happening with the law in Tombstone would reach the Pinkertons, and they'd send one of their agents to sniff around. Once that happens there's no telling what they'll get wind of.'

'What, Court a Pinkerton agent? You seen that man wield a razor?'

'A man learns a trade, doesn't mean he'll stick with it. Would you have that crazy killer Doc Holliday figured as a dentist?'

Craig frowned. 'If you're right about Court, then the killing doesn't stop with Probity.'

'We'll see. I'm hoping his . . . going . . . creates dead ends. Ralf Schäfer's gone. Probity will soon be out of the way, and now we can forget about Annie Schäfer. All right, her body was discovered near Owl Creek mine; that's unfortunate, a stroke of bad luck, but not of our doing and it's not a disaster. In fact, her murder by some unknown crazy could work in our favour. If Court believes we were involved he could go chasing down twisting trails and get lost in a wilderness of wrong leads.'

Craig nodded slowly. 'Yeah, and I've been thinking about Ralf Schäfer, and his talk with Court. The Schäfers saw a wagon running down to the border, saw crates being transferred. Ten to one Schäfer believed that wagon came from Tombstone, and if he told Court, the Pinkerton man'll be off on another lost — '

He broke off. Quaig was no longer listening. He had turned, and was staring down the slope to where the street turned sharply.

'What the hell,' he grated, 'is Deputy Sager playing at, leaving Probity alone in the jail without a guard?'

Craig followed Quaig's gaze. Two men had turned the bend and were walking up the slope, the sound of their boots scraping on the plank walk. One of them was Ulysses Court, the town barber. The other, tall, with a light-coloured Stetson, the glint of a badge on his vest —

'He hasn't,' Craig said tautly. 'That tall man's not Gord Sager, it's John Probity.'

And grasping Ellis Quaig's arm he

43

pulled him back into the shadows and silently drew his six-gun.

★   ★   ★

They crossed the narrow alley that ran alongside the cell where the big deputy lay unconscious, stepped up onto the plank walk and in the night-quiet their boots boomed on the hollow timber. The street sloped upwards. Ahead of them, after fifty yards, there was a sharp turn that put the remaining stretch to the saloon out of sight. They passed the gunsmith's shop with the crude wooden rifle advertising his trade hanging on rusty chains, Buck's Diner where Probity had enjoyed a meal with his sister, and Court cast a wryly amused glance in Probity's direction as they walked under the barber's pole and so on by the small scented room which he had walked out of late that afternoon, almost certainly never to return.

Across the street the livery barn's wide doors were fully open. Despite the late hour, the hostler — an old man who slept but lightly — could be seen at a bench working on a broken harness by the light of a flickering oil lamp. Both men watched him with some interest as they continued walking. Then they reached the bend, rounded it and forgot the old hostler and his night work.

Looking ahead, Probity said quietly, 'Just the two horses. Yours and mine. Everyone's gone home.'

'Not surprising. It was already late when you left the Starlight. I was upstairs in my room over the shop and it was pure luck I was still awake. But I happened to notice Craig and Sager bringing you down the street. That got me interested, so I brewed coffee, thought for a while, then decided to stick my neck out.'

'A hell of a lot's happened since — '

'And it ain't over yet,' Orin Craig snarled.

Shock hit Probity hard. His breath caught in his throat. The marshal had come from nowhere, stepping out of the shadows close enough to touch and smell. He was big and muscular, taut as a bow-string and his face glistened with sweat. His six-gun was levelled, pointing at Probity's belt buckle. The contorted grin and the look of panic in his grey eyes told Probity that he was about to pull the trigger. Fractions of seconds crawled by, as slow and cold as the sleepless hours before dawn. In that time, Probity watched a knuckle whiten on metal, was convinced he saw the six-gun's trigger move.

Galvanized by the will to live, acting without conscious thought, he flung himself sideways into the street. He heard the crack of the shot, felt the bullet tug at his sleeve. Then he rolled and tucked himself tight up against the high plank-walk. He slapped his hand on his Colt .45, whipped it smoothly from its holster, but his position was cramped. His elbow cracked against the timber that was his shield. Pain knifed through his arm. The six-gun flew from his hand. As he cursed and went after it in a flat dive, Orin Craig loomed above him. The big lawman snapped a shot. Dust spurted, and suddenly Probity was blind, pawing desperately at his eyes.

He was flat on his belly. A harsh laugh sent a chill down his spine. He forced open gritty eyelids, twisted around and tried to focus on the lawman while his hand continued to paw the dirt seeking the lost six-gun.

There was a sudden, splintering crack. An exclamation of surprise. A moment's breathless silence. Then a crushing weight landed on his back. All the breath was driven from his lungs. Gasping, he arched his back, brought his knees under him and shook like a dog emerging from a flooded creek. At the same time he swung an elbow backwards and was rewarded by a grunt of pain.

The weight fell away. Probity's eyes were clearing. He saw Orin Craig struggling to rise from where he'd been dumped. Quick as a flash, Probity pivoted on his left hand and swung a vicious kick into the deputy's jaw.

It was enough. Craig collapsed and lay still, one arm flung wide, blood trickling from his open mouth. Probity climbed to his feet, holstered his six-gun and used his bandanna to clear the remains of the dust from his streaming eyes. Then he stepped up onto the plank walk.

Court was watching him, a half-smile on his face. Approval? Maybe, but Probity couldn't have cared less. Craig had been out to kill him, and the only help had come in the nick of time from a rotting plank walk that had splintered and tipped the deputy into the street.

'With two of us,' Probity said bitterly, 'that little dust-up should have been over before it started. I don't much like the idea of riding with a man who waits to see which way the wind's blowing before he makes a move.'

'I stayed where I was most effective,' Court said. 'If our friend here had got involved in the action, you'd be flat on your back waiting for a one-way trip to boot hill.'

And suddenly Probity realized that Court had his six-gun out, pointing almost casually under the flimsy *ramada* where a man was standing in the shadows. Ellis Quaig. And Probity remembered that a short while ago, from his bunk in the cell, he had heard two men leave the jail and suspected then that it was Craig and Quaig.

'In that case, I thank you — though from the looks of him and that fancy six-gun he's got pouched, he's all mouth and no substance.'

The big businessman was as still as death. He was leaning back against the wall. A cigar smouldered between his fingers, and the light from the street lamps glowed red in his eyes.

'Maybe he wields power of a different but especially lethal kind,' Court said softly. 'What do you have to say to that suggestion, Mr Quaig?'

Ellis Quaig said nothing. With a last, unshakeable stare that had the clear intention of fixing Probity and Court in his mind, he flicked the ash from his cigar, pushed away from the wall and set off across the street.

'Kept his mouth tight shut, but let his actions speak volumes,' Court said. 'Treated us with disdain. Didn't give the unconscious town marshal a glance. There, my friend, goes a very dangerous man.'

4

How long does it take to ride a little more than ten miles, at night, across rugged desert terrain?

Not much longer than it takes, Probity figured, for Orin Craig to climb up out of the dust, shake his head and commence working out what the hell had hit him hard enough to break his jaw. And why Ellis Quaig had run for home and left him for dead.

Probity chuckled in the darkness. Riding next to him as they headed south-east from Rawton under a canopy of glittering stars that stretched to unimaginable velvet distances, Ulysses Court glanced across questioningly.

'You find something amusing?'

'Was wondering how you know where Annie lived, but I don't,' Probity said.

'Ralf Schäfer came into the shop, did

some talking while I hacked his hair up off his shoulders.'

'I know about that visit. From what I heard, he discussed possible troubles heading his way, not his domestic arrangements.'

It was Court's turn to laugh.

'He'd said enough to get me interested. I tailed him one day when he was heading home. Stayed well back, then rode around the area where his house is situated to get clear in my mind what he'd been talking about.'

'Not much to understand, not a lot you could find out in broad daylight. A house, a trail, the border. Rumours of a wagon load of silver rolling down from Tombstone. A bunch of Mexicans up to no good. You knew all that before you followed Schäfer. The imponderables are in what lies behind those night operations.'

'Operations?'

'Stands to sense it happened more than once. They get away with smuggling silver one time, they'll do it again.'

'So why didn't your sister tell you about the other times? If they saw it happen once, they'd have been on the alert.'

Probity rode in silence for a moment.

'Let me correct that,' he said after a while. 'Maybe it didn't happen again. But now they're both out of the way, I'd lay odds on it starting up again.'

'That's not certain. It's not a good time to venture into Mexico. You know the country's in turmoil? Or, to put it another way, are you aware that anyone looking remotely suspicious — gringo or Mex, makes no difference — is likely to end up in a rat-infested dungeon without charge, without trial, without much hope of ever again seeing the light of day?'

'Yeah, I know what's going on. Porfirio Díaz stepped down as president, Manuel González is up there in his place. But González and Díaz are as thick as thieves. Juárez would be favourite to take control again, but he's long dead. The campesinos would like

Lerdo de Tejada back in power, but they don't stand a hope in hell. Give it a couple of years and Díaz will be back.'

Probity was conscious of the other man studying him, and felt mildly irritated. No man likes to be kept in the dark, and Ulysses Court was playing his cards close to his chest. Something in his demeanour had drawn Ralf Schäfer to his barber's shop, and Court had followed up Schäfer's story. In the jail, he had handled Deputy Gord Sager like a man used to handling a six-gun, not snipping away with scissors or using a cut-throat razor to scrape a man's whiskers. And now he was admitting trailing Schäfer, when logic suggested an ordinary barber would have listened to the young man's story then promptly forgotten it when the next customer sat in his chair.

'Something tells me,' Probity said, 'that you're not a barber — '

'Not after tonight, I'm not.'

'You never were — or let's say it's been some time since that was your full time occupation. I'll be forever in your debt, but I'd still like to know what manner of man can switch from lathering a feller's jaw to using a six-gun to knock a man senseless.'

'A man playing a part,' Court said.

'Go on.'

'You heard of John Behan?'

'Cochise County sheriff. Not the most popular of men.'

'And suspected of income tax fraud.'

'Really?' Probity shot Court a glance. 'And you're what . . . a tax inspector?'

'I work for the Pinkertons.'

'Is that a fact?' Probity said softly. 'Now, why is it I take that explanation with a very big pinch of salt?'

'I assure you it's absolutely true.'

'Oh, I don't doubt it. Your working for the Pinkertons, I mean. As for the rest of it, the bit about Behan's creative accounting, I can see it happening, but I don't see how that ties in with your riding miles under a blazing sun after a young man who saw a load of silver changing hands in the dead of night.'

'Maybe it's best,' Court said quietly, 'if you don't ask too many questions.'

* * *

'I see two horses dozing in the corral,' Probity said, 'when Annie's house is supposed to be empty.'

They'd drawn rein at a comfortable distance, finding and moving into thin shadows cast by a stand of skeletal trees atop an insignificant knoll, dismounting in the creaking silence and using gentle hands on muzzles to keep their mounts quiet. The house Court had led them to was a single storey timber building, its corrugated iron roof rust-red in the shafts of moonlight that slanted through high, shifting clouds. It was set a couple of hundred yards back from a rough, rutted trail that crossed the stony course of Bronca Creek before running downhill through scrub and tall Saguaro cacti towards the Mexican border. An out-building leaned splintered boards drunkenly against the house's southern wall. The peeled-pole corral, with its two drowsy occupants, was a little way uphill from the house, sheltered by another stand of gnarled trees.

'Oil lamp's lit,' Court mused. 'Whoever's in there could be wide awake, in which case we're in trouble, or out of their minds on tequila or mescal and there for the taking.'

'Your best guess as to identity?'

The Pinkerton man's horse snorted softly as he slipped his Winchester rifle out of its saddle-boot.

'Well, you were correct in saying that Ralf's shooting, followed by Annie's death, left the house empty. If you're also right and they'll now begin moving silver, why not put a couple of their men in there? Use the place as a border HQ for whatever illegal activities're going on here?'

'They? A couple of their men? That's pretty vague. Doesn't sound as if we've got much information to go on.'

'There's one sure way of getting more.'

'Except I'm a peaceable man.'

'Yeah, and I'm the Rawton town barber, dab hand with a razor, always a ready ear for a homily. Come off it, Probity! You worked alongside Earp in Dodge City, that qualifies you for whatever the hell's needed when we . . . well, I'll leave it to you, it's your sister's house, you tell me how we play this.'

Probity sighed. 'We go in on foot, so put your rifle away. Up close, a long gun'll get you all tangled up — and we do need to get close, catch 'em with their flared Mex pants down around their fancy boots. You take the front, I'll take the rear.'

'I can't see a back door.'

'Not needed. I'll wait until you've circled around, reached the front of the house, then put a couple of fast shots through the back window. That'll grab their attention while you bust in through the front door and catch 'em cold.'

Court grinned. His teeth gleamed white in the shadows, but his blue eyes were like chips of ice.

'Two horses doesn't mean two men. There could be half a dozen in there.'

'Well, there's one sure way of finding out,' Probity said, echoing the other man's words, and with a bleak smile he slipped out of the shadows and into the moonlight.

He moved off the knoll first, then held back, watching as Court cut away from him and walked unhurriedly up the slope so that he could swing in around the corral and come at the house downhill. The Pinkerton man moved soundlessly. He picked his way effortlessly through the tangle of low scrub, remaining in full view of anyone watching from the house because he had no choice, yet somehow following the scudding shadows of the drifting clouds so that his shape became just another part of an ever-changing kaleidoscope.

Maxwell Golightly, Probity thought,

recalling his bearded mentor, *would be proud of the Pinkerton agent.*

His own route was direct, but dangerous. It was no more than fifty yards in a straight line to the back wall of the house. Court was looking at the blank face of a stone chimney stack. Probity was walking directly towards two windows, their curtains open. He guessed the window in darkness would be a bedroom. Through the other, as he crept closer, Probity could see into a lamp-lit room that stretched from the back of the house to the front.

But . . . there was no sign of the men who had arrived on horseback. No Mexicans sitting around a table where a blackened oil lamp cast yellow light on a greasy pack of cards, half-empty bottles wreathed in coils of smoke from cheap cigarillos.

As his imagination ran riot, inside Probity a worm of unease stirred.

He stopped his steady advance, aligned himself behind a tall saguaro, looked beyond the corner of the house for Court. The Pinkerton man had reached the far side of the corral, and was turning down the slope. Into danger. There was no cover. As he moved away from the corral, the skies cleared and the area was flooded with pale light. The only shadow was Court's and it followed him, rippling across the rough ground as he crossed the open space. He was moving without haste, but if there was a window alongside the stone chimney in that side wall —

Glass shattered, and was followed instantly by a shot. It was fired from the darkened bedroom window. The muzzle flash and the crack of the detonation were inseparable. The bullet sliced a chunk of green flesh from the saguaro. Sour liquid splashed Probity's face, his mouth. He was spitting as he hit the ground, rubbing his eyes for the second time that night. The second shot kicked dirt into his face. It stuck to the cactus juice. He rolled onto his back and ripped off his bandanna. Somehow the act of wiping his cold wet face got mixed up with the idea of Court the town barber and his hot towels, and suddenly Probity was choking with silent laughter as a third shot ricocheted off a rock and howled into the distance.

Out of the corner of his eye he caught a flash of movement. Court was taking advantage of the commotion, of the surprise attack on Probity. He was charging across the open ground towards the house, six-gun glinting. As Probity sprang to his feet, Court blasted two quick shots, aimed nowhere in particular but intended to keep heads down. When the second rang out, drawing sparks from the tin roof, he had reached the house and was out of sight.

The gunfire from the bedroom window had fallen silent. Probity was standing with his back against the saguaro. Its tough flesh offered scant cover, limited protection. Expecting at any moment another shot to drill straight through the cactus and into his back, he breathed raggedly, futilely tensing his muscles. Gritting his teeth, he eased his six-gun from its holster, hefted its reassuring bulk. Then he took a last deep breath, held it, and exploded from cover.

At once, the gunman in the house opened up. Bullets hissed by Probity's head, plucked at his shirt. But now Probity was running straight at the window. A frontal assault inspires panic. When he was ten feet from the window, Probity caught a glimpse of a face. The black eyes were wide and staring. A six-gun poked through the shattered glass. A dull metallic click was followed by a hoarse Mexican oath.

Probity fired just the once. The shot drilled cleanly and bloodlessly into the back of the gunman's skull as he turned to flee. He fell away, dead before he hit the floor. Without pause, Probity ran for the downhill side of the house. It was in deep shadow. His shoulder hit the sagging outhouse, which had no back wall, an unglazed crude opening for a window at the front. He was knocked sideways by the impact. Recovering, he heard a dull thud followed by a splintering crash. Court, demolishing the front door. The crash was followed by two shots that rang as one. Then Probity was around the house, into the moonlight. He burst in through the heavy door that was now sagging on its hinges.

He saw dark furniture, a fancy oil lamp hanging from a beam, the remains of a meal on the table but no sign of the smashed dishes and pools of spilled liquor and worse that would have fouled the interior had the house been occupied by bandits.

Over his shoulder Court shouted, 'Get a tie, rawhide, anything, this man's bleeding to death.'

He was down on his knees.

Probity was still clutching his bandanna.

He rushed to Court's side and dropped to one knee, twisting the damp cotton into a thin cord. The Pinkerton man had used his knife to slice through the Mexican's trouser leg, then pulled off the man's boot and slipped the severed cloth over his foot. The flesh was exposed. A bullet had torn a terrible, ragged gash in the white flesh of the man's inner thigh. Out of the gaping wound bright red blood pulsed in regular beats. Already there was a wide pool on the dirt floor. Both men were kneeling in it, their trousers soaked to their boots.

Court's hands were slick with blood. His knife lay between his knees. He snatched the makeshift cord from Probity, wrapped it round the wounded man's thigh. Under it he slipped the pad he had formed from the trouser leg. He pressed the pad with his hand, watched the pulsing blood; moved the pad higher. Then he knotted the cord, drew his six-gun and slipped it between the cord and the man's slick skin.

'Is too late,' the Mexican said softly, calmly.

'It's not too late until you're bled white,' Court said, twisting the pistol, watching the cord bite into the flesh, the pad press hard against the unseen artery — without any noticeable effect.

The man smiled. His teeth shone in the gloom.

'The wound, it is too big . . . the bleeding . . . '

His voice faded away weakly. His eyelids fluttered.

Probity, sitting back on his heels, was puzzled. The dying man was no bandit. His ruined clothing — torn, slashed, soaked in blood — was of high quality, and his face showed clearly that he was no peasant, no cross-border thief. For one thing, he was too old: Probity put him in his early sixties. His eyes were grey and intelligent, his face and body lean but from good health and fitness not lack of food, his hair and beard neatly trimmed and edged in grey.

So, a wealthy landowner, an official of some kind in some business or government organisation — or simply a gentleman road agent who cared for his appearance?

'Sir,' Probity said, 'what are you doing here, in this situation?'

Court, bloody hands on the twisted bandanna, flashed him a glance then shook his head. He understood what Probity was getting at, but knew they were losing the man. If there was a mystery, the answer was going to die with him.

'Not . . . enough . . . '

The words were whispered. Probity leaned closer.

'I'm sorry?'

'For her . . . it is not yet enough . . . '

'Sir, all I can see is your countrymen taking silver that doesn't belong to them,' Probity said. 'The advice I'd give them — '

The man's sudden chuckle became a choking cough. The strain on his body forced a gush of blood from his leg, but the blood was tinged with pink froth and the gush became a trickle.

'They are doing that, yes, but I tell you it is not yet enough . . . and you, you put it simply and think you understand . . . but you know . . . noth-ing . . . '

The words trailed away. The effort to enunciate clearly and precisely what was important to him was too much; too much for a body that was almost drained of blood. He died without sound, without movement. He was there, then gone, and for some reason Probity felt a haunting sense of loss.

'He's gone, but it's not over,' Court said. 'I don't know if you been listening, but there's a rider coming hell-for-leather down the trail.'

5

The room was a slaughterhouse patterned in light and shade. Pools of wet blood on the floor caught the moonlight spilling in through the broken door. That light was reflected upwards into the faces of the two men, turning them into hollow-eyed ghouls. The dead man on the floor seemed to have lost all bulk, and cast a thin flat shadow. He could have been sleeping, but no man would have chosen such a bed. With a last glance at him, knowing nothing could be done to clean up the mess, Probity and Court ran for the open air with guns drawn, themselves looking like men who had cut the throats of a dozen steers and happily rolled in the gore.

There was no time to run for alternative cover. A plume of dust from the approaching horse's flashing hoofs was already drifting across the corral where the two horses were awake and trotting towards the rail with ears pricked. As they whinnied a welcome the rider spun the horse in off the trail, pushed it the two hundred yards or so up the narrow track leading to the house and dragged the chestnut pony to a sliding halt almost in front of the two watching men.

'Well, well,' Ulysses Court said. 'What have we here?'

The young woman who threw herself from the saddle was slim and blonde, long hair tumbling around strong shoulders. She was dressed in a cotton shirt, the sleeves pushed back, her dark trousers tucked into scuffed leather boots. A blue neckerchief was a splash of bright colour at her throat. It matched exactly the searing intensity of her eyes, which were that eternal paradox: the icy blue of the hottest of flames.

'I don't know what I expected,' she said, 'but it certainly wasn't this. It's the middle of the night, and I find two men turning my brother's house into a butcher's shop.'

'Your brother?' Probity said, eyebrow raised.

'Ralf Schäfer. I'm Sabine, so you can put away your guns.' She shrugged. 'OK, so he's dead, which means the place belongs to his wife. Only now she's dead, buried this morning. So, take a guess at who's the new owner?'

'I'd say, in Arizona territory, it's the person who gets here first and takes possession.'

'No.' She shook her head fiercely. 'Ralf did things right. Bought the place for cash, kept the deeds in a bank safe in Tombstone. That means ownership passes to next of kin — and that's me.'

'You think so? If I had a mind, you could have a legal battle on your hands.' Probity nodded slowly.

'Annie never told me she had a sister-in-law.'

A faint smile curled the young woman's lips.

'I knew she had a brother, but she neglected to tell me he was riding to save her on his big white stallion.' She tilted her head. 'So you're John Probity?'

Probity nodded. 'And this is Ulysses Court. Ulysses has been working as Rawton town barber, but . . . '

And now the woman's faint smile became a barely suppressed grin. 'But he got a bit careless with his razor.' She looked them up and down, taking in pants that were dark with blood from the knees down. 'I take it you're not going to invite me in?'

'Not unless you want to lose your supper.'

'I work in the Oriental, in Tombstone, give Wyatt Earp a hand with faro. I've seen some sickening, gruesome sights, none more so than when my brother Ralf was shot dead across the street outside the Golden Eagle.' She paused. 'Dead Mexicans,' she said softly, but with great perception, 'are as entitled as anyone to a decent burial.'

Court spoke for the first time.

'Let's get to it, then,' he said. 'Young lady, I suggest you bring your gloves.'

* * *

The coffee was scalding hot, and strong, which was perhaps just as well because the rich aroma masked any lingering smells of Mexican blood. It had taken them two hours to clean up after the slaughter and bury the two men, with Sabine doing more than pull her weight. She was familiar with the house and could direct the way to the tools needed to dig graves in the bone-dry earth, the hard brushes and rags required to scrub the floor in the living room where the elderly Mexican of breeding had bled to death.

The house had been empty for just a few hours after Annie's death and, as the two Mexicans had died before they'd had time to leave their mark, there was no shortage of basic supplies. When the gruesome work was finished, when three horses had been unsaddled and set loose in the corral with the dead Mexican's mounts, Probity, Court and Sabine Schäfer had all lent a hand in preparing a hot meal. That had been eaten ravenously, and in silence. Now, with coffee being enjoyed in the comfort of Ralf and Annie's worn easy chairs and by the warm light of a single brass oil lamp, it was time for talk.

'Thirty-five miles,' Probity said, 'is a long ride for a young woman to make, at night, and for no reason.'

'I've already explained. I got news of Annie's death, and rushed to claim my property.' She lifted her hands defensively as Probity registered his silent objection with a grimace and a shake of the head. 'Yes, maybe I was hasty in assuming ownership, but as quickly as I moved to get here I was way too slow.'

'That's because the men who moved in ahead of you didn't need to wait for news that Annie was dead,' Probity said. 'They, or their business associates, committed the murder.'

Sabine shook her head. 'No, that's not right.'

'Of course it is — '

'Annie worked with me — did you know that?'

Probity frowned. 'In a saloon?'

'It was perfectly respectable. She'd been in the job just a couple of days, and intended to bunk in my room over the Oriental during the week, come home to Ralf at the weekends.'

'What about Ralf? What did he do?'

'He was some kind of engineer. So in that respect he was involved with the silver mines.' She shrugged. 'I don't know . . . maybe that's what made him smell a rat.'

'Never mind that, for the moment,' Court said. 'You were saying you don't believe the Mexicans were involved in Annie's death. Why not?'

Sabine smiled wryly. 'You're a woman, you're working in a saloon, so you get a label: you're a working girl, and fair game. Just a couple of days into the job and already Annie was getting pestered by one of the Clanton boys.'

'Ike?'

'No, the younger one, Billy.'

Court grunted his disgust. 'Both of them are more than capable of murdering a woman when they're not fighting with the Earps.' He paused, drank some coffee, his brow furrowed in thought. 'Where did Ralf work?'

'Owl Creek mine.'

'So if that wagon he and Annie saw at the border came from Owl Creek,' Probity said, 'he'd have recognized it?'

'It didn't.' Sabine shook her head. 'Afterwards, Ralf spoke to Ronan Casey. Not only that, in the time he had left Ralf asked questions elsewhere. Didn't make a scrap of difference, he was no closer to finding out . . . '

'And then he died,' Probity said quietly as Sabine's words trailed off and she stared intently at precious memories locked inside her head.

'And then he was murdered,' she corrected huskily.

'In his case there's not much doubt

why,' Court said. 'First he's seen watching the wagon in the dead of night, then he starts looking for answers.'

'Which is exactly what I'm going to do,' Sabine said.

'I'd advise against it.'

'Really? And what gives you that right?'

Court sighed. 'I was telling Probity that I work for the Pinkertons — '

'Well, hallelujah,' Sabine cut in, 'I've got expert help.' She flicked a glance at Probity. 'What about you? I'm pretty certain Annie's death's not connected, but are you in or out?'

It was Court who answered. 'Probity's in for one very good reason: if he doesn't get to the bottom of this, he too could wind up dead. She may not have died for that reason, but Annie was there at the border with Ralf and saw that wagon. With Ralf gone she was on her own, out on a limb . . . '

He broke off, frowning. 'You worked with Annie. Surely she must have discussed this with you?'

'A hint here and there. She mentioned seeing a wagon on a clear night, Mexicans, something about silver being taken across the border and a pretty clear threat — and that's about it. When Ralf was murdered, she was a very frightened young woman. I could see that, but not what she intended to do about it. She could have gone to Sheriff Behan — but who the hell trusts him?'

'Yeah, well, what she did was send for Probity. To certain people in Rawton, that makes Probity's position crystal clear: there's a possibility he knows too much, and for that reason he has to be removed.'

Sabine pursed her lips. 'Do I detect an undercurrent here? Is there something special about Mr Probity that makes him a real danger to these unknown villains?'

Probity smiled. 'Maybe what concerns them is not what I know, but who I know, and the first person I intend talking to is your boss, Wyatt Earp.'

6

It was, Probity decided, a waste of time trying to sleep. He and Court had gallantly left Ralf and Annie's comparatively unspoiled bedroom to Sabine Schäfer, and when she had retired for what was left of the night they enjoyed a final cigarette, then unrolled their blankets and bedded down on the living-room floor. But despite all the scrubbing they had done, the smell of tobacco wasn't strong enough to hide the stink of raw blood. The shifting light, creating eerie patterns on the walls as clouds drifted across the face of the moon, brought ghosts moaning out of the shadows as soon as Probity's eyelids began to droop.

Casting an envious glance at the snoring Pinkerton man, he gathered his blankets and trailed them carelessly out through the broken door. There, where the air reeked of nothing worse than desert dust and parched vegetation, and the hard-packed earth even at that hour retained the afterglow of the previous day's heat, he finally drifted off into uneasy slumber.

He was dragged out of thick, clogged unconsciousness by the murmur of voices and the smell of frying bacon. When he yawned, scrubbed his eyes with his knuckles and squinted through the raised arms of the tall saguaros to the eastern horizon he reckoned it was still an hour before dawn. He must have slept for, what, two hours at the most? His ears were buzzing. The wound slashed by Gord Sager's six-gun had scabbed over, but was still painful and his head throbbed.

Then his mind cleared, and alarm bells started ringing. Full daylight could bring an armed posse hammering down the trail from Rawton. He had been accused of murder, broken out of jail, then kicked the town marshal unconscious in a knock-down, bruising fight in the main street dust. He could have his neck stretched for any one of those offences, with Court swinging alongside him for cracking a deputy's skull with his six-gun, locking him in a cell, and helping the prisoner to escape.

As he rolled out of his blankets with a half-stifled groan, reached for his gun-belt and hobbled into the house for his breakfast, Probity couldn't keep his aching face from splitting in a wry grin.

Looked at that way, today could only get better.

★ ★ ★

'I've reached the conclusion, after considerable thought,' Ulysses Court said, 'that after a couple of hours' restless sleep, Ellis Quaig and his lawmen cronies in Rawton will have cooled down enough to realize they acted with rare stupidity.'

'Drawing too much attention to themselves, when they're playing a game that requires secrecy?'

'That's one big reason — although Christ knows what that game is.'

'The other is that they were wasting their time, because I know nothing that could cause them any harm, or disrupt their plans.'

'Exactly. Poor, frightened Annie had nothing to tell you. Furthermore, accusing you of raping and murdering your own sister was a charge that was never going to stick, and could even backfire in a most horrendous way.'

Sabine had pushed her empty plate away with a clatter, and was nodding.

'If I'd seen Billy Clanton sniffing around Annie, stands to sense the whole damn town of Tombstone would have been talking of nothing else.'

'And even if Billy had nothing to do with it, it's always possible Sheriff John Behan or the Earps will come up with the real killer,' Court said, 'leaving Craig and his deputy in Rawton looking like fools. No, take my word for it, Probity, in the cold light of day they'll realize their mistake and drop you like a hot potato.'

'Well, they certainly achieved one thing,' Probity said. 'I got out of Rawton a hell of a sight faster than I rode in.'

'And despite what you said last night about who you know, you're free to keep on going,' Sabine said. 'If Annie's death had nothing to do with what she saw here that night, there's nothing keeping you.'

'Except the desire to see her killer brought to justice.' He shrugged helplessly. 'Besides, what Annie saw here at the border frightened her half to death, led to her husband's death, and had ruined her life even if she'd lived. And Ralf Schäfer was my brother-in-law. I didn't know the man, had never met him, but that doesn't remove from me the obligation to find out why he was murdered, and avenge his death.'

'Your brother-in-law, my brother.' Sabine's voice had softened. Her eyes were again suspiciously moist. 'So you're not going to turn your back on this, you'll come with me to Tombstone, talk to Wyatt Earp?'

'Those men in Rawton treated me like a rogue steer, used my face for a punch bag, left their mark.' For an instant Probity let his anger show. Then he drew a breath, and nodded. 'Yes, of course. If I'm still a free man at the end of the day, then I'm with you.'

'Have you not been listening?' Court said. He was shaking his head as he rose from the breakfast table. 'You're small fry, Probity. There'll be no posse, you're the forgotten man — and that can only work in your favour. Ride as soon as we're finished here. A steady pace will see you in Tombstone some time after midday. You can then choose to talk to Earp at once, in his capacity as deputy US Marshal, or wait until the sun goes down and go with Sabine to the Oriental where he'll be working the box at the faro table.'

'And you?'

'If you're their forgotten man, I'm

the thorn in their side, and I'll make sure word gets around Rawton that I'm a Pinkerton man.' Court grinned. 'They can believe it or not, but there's always the possibility that it could be true. That will not only make Quaig and his cronies back off, it'll pull the customers into my barber's chair — and with my new-found fame I reckon it'll take a lathered shaving brush thrust into their open mouths to stop them talking their heads off.'

7

Tombstone's streets, despite the town's location in the hills as the hub of the area's silver mines, were broad and flat. At eight that night they were almost deserted, rutted expanses of dried mud dimly lit by oil lamps hanging from rusting brackets on the buildings' false fronts. A piano heard tinkling inside the Oriental Saloon might have attracted passers-by, if there had been any. Inside the big room there was the occasional burst of conversation and some laughter from the half-a-dozen drinkers on the premises, but that early in the evening the place was about as lively as the nearby undertaker's parlour.

When John Probity walked into the saloon, the first person he saw was Sabine Schäfer. Her red silk dress was a flame flickering brightly amid the drab blacks and brown's of the men's clothing as she moved restlessly, her blonde hair — loose about her shoulders — a moving shimmer of gold that was in sharp contrast to the thick black hair and drooping moustache of the man who sat in front of her.

Wyatt Earp was seated in the banker's cutout at the deserted faro table. He was dressed in a black frock coat, a string tie of the same colour emphasising the pure white of his shirt. He was sitting back in his chair, smoking a cigar, idly playing against himself by turning the cards in the shoe and moving chips across the layout according to a win or loss.

He looked up when Probity walked in. Recognition was instantaneous. He gave the cards a final flick with his finger, turned and said something to Sabine, then left his cigar in an ashtray on the table and crossed to the bar.

'Been a long time, John,' he said as Probity joined him. 'You were still in Dodge City when I left, still wearing a badge. I know dodging bullets fired by drunken cowboys celebrating successful cattle drives come up all the way from southern Texas can get a mite wearisome, but why end up here? Why Arizona? And how is it the first place you walk into is my saloon?'

'You own this place?'

Earp rocked his head, as if unsure of the right answer.

'Well, that was a mite presumptuous. My main occupation in here is dealing faro. Luke Short's ridden God knows how many miles down from Leadville, Colorado, to lend a hand. You might say he's helping me relieve optimistic suckers of their hard-earned dollars.'

'Through a rigged faro shoe?'

'If anyone else had said that, I'd certainly take exception. I make damn sure the game's clean, John, because I've got a quarter share in the faro concession — and I guess you know I'm deputy US marshal.'

He crooked a finger. A shot glass of whiskey came sliding along the bar. Earp pushed it towards Probity who picked it up, drained it, grimaced.

'Then in your capacity as a Tombstone lawman,' Probity said, 'you'll be looking into the death of that girl who was found ... I think it was at Owl Creek mine?'

Earp touched his moustache, frowned, gestured to the barman for a drink for himself. When it arrived he tasted it before speaking, then nodded slowly.

'Annie Schäfer,' he said. 'Yes, you're right, workers taking a break came across her body near Ronan Casey's place.' He looked over his glass at Probity, his eyes thoughtful. 'If you know that, you'll also know that her man was a mining engineer. Ralf Schäfer. And that a drunk waving a pistol gunned him down on the corner of Fifth and Allen — just across the way.'

He said no more, seemingly content to stand with his back to the bar as Probity gathered his thoughts. But Probity was taking his time, choosing his words with care. Opting for caution, he waved a hand vaguely.

'You see a connection?'

'Ralf and his wife?' Earp shrugged. 'They were married. Now they're both dead. Other than that . . . '

Probity smiled. 'You always were a cagey customer — '

'What do you want me to say, John?'

'How about this? That rumour has it the Schäfers saw something down at the border that signed their death warrants? That what they saw involved . . . the movement of silver, from Tombstone all the way down the trail that leads into Mexico.'

'Movement?' Earp smiled crookedly. 'Now who's being cagey?' He lifted his glass, saw it was empty, placed it on the bar. 'Anyway, consider it said. That's one of many rumours flying around. I don't pay them much heed. But that one, being unusual because it has implications more serious than cattle rustling or stage coach robbery, has been looked into. And found to be groundless.'

'You saying it didn't happen?'

'Not to my knowledge.'

'Which is based on . . . ?'

'Asking around. Talking to mine owners who should know if someone's stealing their ore.'

'But are unlikely to tell you if they themselves are involved in a little cross-border smuggling.'

'You think they'd increase their income that way?' Earp pulled a face. 'I think they'd lose on that kind of deal, wouldn't be worth their while, wouldn't be worth the risk. Hell, they move a wagon load down to the border, at night, an ambush is a red hot certainty and they'd end up with nothing.'

'Ralf Schäfer was an intelligent man. He knows what he saw.'

'Yeah, and he worked at Owl Creek, where I went to talk to Ronan Casey because — '

'Because that's where my sister's body was found.'

'Jesus Christ, John, your *sister?* Is that right? Is that what this is about?'

'Indirectly. She sent for me. I wasn't much help.' Probity hesitated, then changed tack. 'We've been talking about the Schäfers, we've been talking about the illegal movement of silver, but you haven't yet mentioned the young lady standing at the faro table.'

'No, and you haven't told me what happened to your face. You taken to brawling in your old age?'

'Never mind my face. What if I tell you that late last night that young lady helped bury two Mexicans down at the Schäfers' house? Which stands within spitting distance of the border mentioned in that rumour you say has no substance.'

'The only reason that story surprises me is that it was Sabine helping dig the graves. The house was standing empty, John. Mexicans are heavily involved in the cross-border smuggling of cattle, alcohol, tobacco. Fights are common, deaths not unusual.'

'One man bled to death. He was clearly a Mexican of breeding. I think his involvement is something else that should surprise you. Because surely his presence there suggests something more important than the movement of maverick steers or a few jugs of bootleg liquor?'

For a few moments the two men were silent. The faint snap of playing cards could be heard. A gambler, thin almost to emaciation, had crossed the room and was sitting at the faro table. Sabine was acting as dealer in Earp's absence.

'Doc Holliday,' Earp said quietly, and nodded at the thin man. 'Remember him in Dodge?'

'Sure. He was there when you and I were working under Marshal Charlie Bassett. A sick man, but he covered your back more than once.'

'And he'll need to do it again. Old Man Clanton's boys are stirring up trouble, Tom and Frank McLaury are spoiling for a fight and alongside them there's Billy Claiborne. The whole bunch hangs out at Old Man Clanton's ranch on the San Pedro — some five miles north of Charleston, less than an hour's ride from Tombstone. Billy's over at the bar now, with Ike Clanton. The two men closest to us. Fix them in your memory, John. They're crazy from birth, trouble, both of them, and isn't that what you go looking for?'

The two men Earp indicated were of medium height, both with thick dark hair. Clanton's was curly. His face was fleshy, and he sported a drooping moustache. Claiborne was much leaner. His hair was slicked back, his face somewhat pinched, with a broad forehead and a pointed chin.

Claiborne sensed Probity's stare. He turned his head, met Probity's gaze, held it for a moment then turned away and said something to Ike Clanton.

Earp chuckled. 'I guess it's the other way around. You're with me, and that maybe gives you a reputation you don't deserve. Could be that trouble you're looking for will come sooner than you expect.'

'What I'm looking for is something I'm clearly not going to get from you. Sure, sure, I understand, you're a busy man, beset from all sides — '

'You didn't ask me about the other rumours, John.' Earp stroked his moustache, looked steadily at Probity. 'I like the one about the man who broke out of Rawton jail with the help of the town barber. Now, the sensible thing to do in that situation would be to get out of town in a hurry — wouldn't you say?'

'I'm sure he did.'

'Oh, no. What he did was stay behind for while, because he was bearing a grudge, burning up with anger. With this barber to back him up, he hid in an alley and waylaid — you know, I love that word — he waylaid the town marshal, a real decent feller called Orin Craig who was setting off in pursuit. Without saying one damn word this escapee starts a fight right there in the street — covered by his barber friend's six-gun — and finishes it by kicking that lawman to death.'

PART TWO

8

For John Probity, being wanted for murder was a situation not covered by trapper Maxwell Golightly's philosophy. It was, Probity decided as he rolled out of bed the next morning, the worst imaginable example of a man being caught with his pants down — more especially so as he knew damned well that it would have taken more than a kick in the jaw to kill a man as tough as Orin Craig.

Craig had been alive when Probity and Court rode out of Rawton. Unconscious, but breathing — possibly through a broken nose, but that wouldn't have been for the first time in a western lawman's career. So the second thought that occurred to Probity as he ruminated on his new-found criminal status, was, why hadn't they kept a closer eye on Ellis Quaig?

Quaig, in Court's estimation, was dangerous. According to Court, he had been strangely subdued during the fight and, as Probity had witnessed, he had ventured not a word of any kind in its aftermath. Instead, he had fixed both Probity and Court with a venomous glare, then walked off down the street trailing smoke from his cigar.

In Probity's opinion — backed up by Wyatt Earp's statement — Marshal Orin Craig was a basically decent man who last night had panicked; if there was a rotten apple in the Rawton marshal's office, it was Gord Sager. That might align Sager with Ellis Quaig — if Probity and Court were right in their feeling that Quaig was dangerous, possibly crooked. From that position it was easy to imagine Quaig walking down Rawton's main street, releasing the dazed and angry Gord Sager from the cell, and getting him to finish off Orin Craig.

Is that what had happened? And if so, why?

What the hell was Ellis Quaig's game

— and what, if anything, did it have to do with the movement of silver ore across the Mexican border?

Probity had spent the night in a room above the Golden Eagle Brewery. He dressed quickly, ran down the stairs and nodded to a couple of men who were swabbing the bars and sweeping floors, crossed Allen Street, breakfasted in a café that overlooked the Oriental, and was no closer to an answer when he banged the door behind him and began walking the block-and-a-half up Allen Street that would take him to the Old Kindersley Corral where he had left his horse overnight.

Sabine Schäfer worked late nights in her job at the Oriental, so was free for most of every day. Probity had arranged to meet the young woman at the OK Corral, which was where she stabled her chestnut pony.

From there they were heading out to the Owl Creek mine in the hope of finding Ronan Casey with half-an-hour to spare, and a willingness to talk.

* * *

Sabine knew the way to the mine because of her brother's work. It took them an hour to reach it, and it wasn't an easy ride. Already at that hour — a little after ten — the sun was beating down with savage intensity. The hills around Tombstone were barren brown slopes without any shade, and frequently the two riders found themselves allowing their mounts to pick their own route through the detritus of disused workings where the frantic search for the precious ore had proved futile. Dust rose in clouds. Sabine had her blue bandanna pulled high to cover her mouth. Probity couldn't resist a smile as she cursed under her breath in a gentle, ladylike manner.

Owl Creek was located several hundred feet up the western flank of yet another barren hillside in the foothills of the Dragoon Mountains. Its buildings seemed to have been erected as and when required, alongside tracks that wandered hither and yon but seemed to lead nowhere. They were directed by a helmeted worker to a shack that stood almost in the shade of skeletal timber erections with huge, slowly turning wheels that drew oily steel cables from the depths of the earth.

Inside the office, a powerful man with a shock of red hair was standing looking out of a side window. Well over six feet tall, he seemed so deep in thought he did not hear them enter. The door clicked shut. He started, turned, opened his mouth to speak then smiled a little sadly when he saw Sabine.

'I was just thinking about your brother, wondering where we go from here,' he said, walking over to grasp her shoulders and plant a kiss on her cheek. He spoke softly, with a strong Irish lilt. 'What a loss that was. You know it's taking me time to find a man of the right calibre to replace him? And then on top of that, the second tragedy of your sister-in-law's cruel passing, which must surely have knocked you sideways.'

Still holding her shoulders, he looked into her eyes and shook his head in sorrow. Then, releasing her, he gestured to hard chairs, waited until they were both settled then sat in the chair behind the desk.

He looked pleasantly at Probity, then questioningly at Sabine.

'Mr Casey, this is John Probity,' Sabine said. 'John is Annie's brother.'

'My God, so there's tragedy for you too,' Casey said softly. He was looking with compassion at Probity, but beneath that obviously genuine emotion there was also considerable interest. 'You've been staying in Rawton, I believe. It's possible then that you have come across a man by the name of Sager. Gord Sager.'

'I have — but how did you know I'm from Rawton?'

'There's no hidden meaning in my question. It's just that word travels fast in this corner of Cochise county, and as you are from there I was wondering how Sager is getting on in his new job.'

'Well enough, I'd say,' Probity said cautiously. 'From the looks of him he'll be able to handle whatever trouble comes his way.'

'Oh, he's a hard man all right,' Casey said. 'He worked here at Owl Creek until a month ago. I tell you, the hard-rock miners I employ steered well clear of him. I was sorry to lose him, but of course, when he heard about the deputy job coming vacant over in Rawton . . . '

Casey let the silence settle, then said, 'And you, Mr Probity, you are here to . . . what? Ask me if I know anything about the brutal murder of your sister? The answer, unfortunately, is no. It was as much a shock — '

'I'm sure it was,' Probity cut in, 'but that's not why I'm here.'

'Is it not?'

There was a sudden wariness in Casey's tone. The compassion had left his eyes, Probity noticed. The warm blue of a summer lake had been replaced by the glitter of ice.

'Ralf Schäfer saw a wagon at the border. He believed it was moving silver. Annie was convinced that what they both saw that night led to Ralf's death.' Probity paused. 'Was that wagon one of yours?'

'There was no wagon.'

'Two reliable witnesses saw it.'

'They were mistaken.'

'And now they're both dead. Is that convenient?'

Casey glared. 'It's a double tragedy. The two deaths are not connected. As for what happened at the border, I cannot comment. Ralf talked to me. He told me what he had seen — '

'You just said he saw nothing.'

'You misunderstood. What I meant was that the wagon he saw did not come from Owl Creek, or any of the other mines.'

'You can't know that.'

'I'm a businessman. You're suggesting silver ore is being taken across the border for profit. I'm telling you it doesn't happen, because such acts would result in a loss.'

Probity frowned. 'I don't understand.'

Casey's confidence had returned.

He said, 'Anyone taking silver ore across the border into Mexico is delivering nothing more than a wagon load of rocks. You understand? For those rocks to be of any use, of any value, they must be taken to a processing plant where the silver will be extracted. We are talking about a long-term project of considerable magnitude. And that doesn't make sense, does it now, because all cross-border smugglers are after is a fast buck.'

'Then what did Ralf see?'

Casey shook his head. 'All I can tell you is what he didn't see. And what he saw at the border that night was most assuredly not a wagon loaded with silver ore from this or any other of the Tombstone mines.'

★ ★ ★

'You didn't notice it, did you?'

They were riding abreast down a long gradient some distance from the Owl Creek mine, already sweltering in the heat beating down from a cloudless white sky. The track was leading them close to yet more disused mine workings. Rotting, tumbledown shacks stinking of old oil and chemicals were half-buried in steep slopes of rock spoil, removed from the tunnels and dumped. Coils of frayed steel cable and twisted metal sheets as sharp and dangerous as exposed razors lay in wait for the unwary.

Sabine pulled a face. Still waiting for an answer from Probity, she spoke to the chestnut pony, shook the reins and guided it away from danger and onto the rough grassy slope that fell away from the trail. Probity followed, leaning back in the saddle, his mind so occupied he was scarcely aware of what he was doing.

He had been silent since leaving Casey's office. It had quickly become clear to him that if the mine owner had been speaking the truth, it changed everything, left Probity with an impossible task. If there were no quick profits to be made smuggling silver ore, across the border or anywhere else for that matter, then Ronan Casey was right: it wasn't happening.

All right, the big Irishman had half-admitted that there was *something* going on. What John Probity could not understand was why Ralf Schäfer, an experienced mining engineer, had so easily jumped to the wrong conclusion.

And the answer to that was, perhaps he hadn't; or, if he had, then he had quickly realized his mistake, but had been gunned down before he could start asking the right questions.

Probity looked across at Sabine.

'Sorry, what did you say?'

'I said you didn't notice, did you?'

'Didn't notice what?'

'The tintype on Casey's desk. I felt sure you would. I kept expecting you to ask him if he was married.'

'What . . . it was a picture of a woman?'

'More than that,' Sabine said. 'It was a picture of a Mexican woman. I wouldn't have noticed it myself, but for Casey's expression. I caught him looking at the image. The emotions on his face were quite amazing: love, anger, fear, determination; all of those, one after the other.'

'Is the fact that she's Mexican supposed to carry some special meaning? Tombstone, Rawton, Charleston — they're all towns close to the Mexican border. I'd imagine there are a lot of men hereabouts who have taken Mexican wives — and the other way about.'

'Of course,' Sabine said. 'But how many of them are men who own a silver mine? Men who you suspect of being involved in some kind of illegal activity?'

'Hasn't Casey just proved us wrong?'

'He was very convincing.'

'Then . . . ?'

'My brother was convincing, too, and I know who I prefer to belie — '

She broke off with shocked grunt. The wind had been knocked out of her. Slumping forward, her soft moan instantly stifled, she toppled from her horse. In the same instant her fall was explained by the flat, hard crack of a rifle. The crisp, clear sound vibrated musically in the discarded metal sheets. A second shot rang out, hard on the heels of the first. Probity instinctively threw himself from the saddle. He clearly felt the cold wind of the bullet as it sliced through the air close to his scalp. He hit the ground hard. Fingers clawing the coarse grass, he lay flat and still. He was breathing in harsh gasps, adrenaline coursing through his veins. His mind was racing, registering impressions both seen and heard.

Sabine appeared to have been hit dead centre. She had fallen in that silent, leaden way that told Probity she was beyond help. A glance sideways left him feeling sick: her eyes were open, staring sightlessly into the searing light of the sun.

For the sound of the shot to raise harmonics in the rusting metal, it had to have come from close by. That suggested the disused mine workings. Had there been a flash of light a fraction of a second before Sabine took the bullet? Yes, there had. Probity had seen it out of the corner of his eye, had dismissed it as a reflection from broken glass. There was a more substantial timber building further up the slope. That was where the light had flared, in a gap between warped boards. The shot had come from there.

To run those thoughts through his mind took Probity the blink of an eye. Now he was able to take stock of his situation, and he knew he was in trouble. Both horses had taken off as the shot cracked and their riders hit the ground. His rifle had gone with his roan. The roan and Sabine's chestnut had trotted away down the slope, slowing after thirty or forty yards.

Together now, they were standing stock still. Their ears were pricked, their eyes showing the whites as they looked up the hill with flaring nostrils.

The direction of their nervous gaze confirmed Probity's suspicions, and his fears.

Where he was holed up, the gunman had enough cover to stay hidden for a week. And he had a rifle. Probity had nothing but his six-gun, and the slope of the ground that at best made him a difficult target.

But — maybe his reactions had given him a chance. He had hit the ground, and not moved. Played dead — although that hadn't been in his mind. Nevertheless, those long moments of stunned inactivity would have sent an encouraging message to the man squinting out of the shadows into the intense light. Looking along the barrel of his rifle, everything in front of him shimmering in the heat, he would have observed that neither the man nor the woman had moved. That would tell him that both his shots had hit home. His victims were dead.

But to make absolutely sure, he would wait. And watch. So it was a question of which of them could wait the longer. And at that thought Probity allowed himself a thin smile. Face down, he forced himself to relax. Released the tension in his muscles, one by one. Let his breathing slow. He could lie there indefinitely, although — and this would be a problem — in time the sun, beating down on his motionless body, would cause him severe distress.

He had lost his hat. Already the skin at the nape of his neck was burning. His clothing, from neck to ankles, felt as if it was on fire. Very quickly that enclosed heat would draw all moisture from his body, taking with it his strength. He licked his lips, tasted salt — clutched the grass and wondered how long he could hold out —

Someone coughed. Spat. Up the slope. Then there was the clear sound of dry wood splintering. It was followed by the frightened snort of a horse, a muted oath — then the sounds of a horse walking, the quickening rattle of hoofs. Swelling — then fading. The gunman had been forced to ride a little way down the hill to get clear of the ruined shacks, the dumped equipment. Then he had turned his horse, as far as Probity could judge, in the direction of the Owl Creek mine.

The waiting was over. He was still alive.

With a feeling of intense jubilation, mixed with draining sadness, John Probity sprang to his feet and stared up the hill at the drift of dust marking the gunman's passing.

He recalled suggesting to Sabine that Ronan Casey had been convincing. She had been scathing, and quite clear that she preferred her brother's version of events. Nothing was yet proven, but for the ambush to have come so soon after their visit to the mine was stretching coincidence a little too far.

Ronan Casey had some explaining to do.

9

The fact that very few people turned their heads to watch when John Probity rode into Tombstone with Sabine Schäfer's limp body roped face down across the chestnut's saddle said a lot about the town. None of it was complimentary.

It was with a feeling of utter disgust that he cut through Fifth Street to Fremont and there pulled into the undertakers with his grisly burden. A lean man in a black suit came out into the sun to stare impassively. Without a word, he walked to the chestnut and began untying the ropes. That done, Probity helped him carry Sabine inside the single-storey building and lay her on a scrubbed table, asked for her to be buried close to Annie Schäfer, her sister-in-law. He gave his name when payment was queried.

From there he led the chestnut pony to the OK Corral on Allen Street, told the hostler that if he could sell it, he could keep the money. He left his own horse in the comparative cool of the runway, asked for it to be fed, watered and rubbed down in the next half-hour, and handed the hostler a silver coin in payment. Then he walked out into the blistering heat and hesitated, uncertain which direction to take.

The courthouse and jail were in one impressive building on the corner of Third and Toughnut. That was but a short walk away, but would he find Deputy Marshal Earp there? Midweek, a working day, it seemed the logical place to look. But Wyatt Earp was not the average small-town lawman. Something told Probity that the man's faro concession at the Oriental would occupy his mind far more than any notion of keeping the peace, and that conviction gave him his answer.

Dodging a couple of wagons, pulled by lathered teams of mules raising choking clouds of dust through town on their way to one or other of the silver mines, Probity hitched up his gun-belt and made his way back along Allen Street to the Oriental Saloon.

It was midday. Shutters outside the windows had been closed in a vain attempt to keep the place cool. Light was filtering in through cracks and fissures, and flooding through the open door of a room at the far end of the long bar. Dust motes floated in the shafts of light. A barman was tinkling glasses, which caught sparkling highlights on their rims as he wiped them with the end of his soiled apron. The sunlight pouring in from the back room was casting long shadows — tables, chairs, the high bar — and in the reflected light the man in the black overcoat at one of the tables, slowly turning playing cards in a game of solitaire, looked like a corpse.

It was Doc Holliday. A sawn-off shotgun lay across the table next to a half-full shot glass and a blood-stained handkerchief. He looked up, stared at Probity with eyes that shone with an unhealthy lustre. Seeing nothing to interest him, he returned to his game and snapped another card on the layout.

Then one of the long shadows raced across the floor and became impossibly elongated, and Probity turned as Wyatt Earp emerged from the back room.

'You just missed Rawton's new marshal,' Earp said, eyes penetrating under his dark brows. 'Was in here looking for that feller I told you about, beat Orin Craig to death. Though not with too much urgency. He knows damn well, the feller's got any sense he'll be halfway across Texas.'

'Could be his first mistake. The new marshal have a name?'

'Gord Sager.'

'That's the second time I've heard that name today,' Probity said. 'Ronan Casey told me Sager used to work at Owl Creek mine.'

'That he did,' Earp said. He glanced

across at Doc Holliday, let his eyes take in the shotgun, then returned his gaze to Probity. 'But what were you doing out there? You figuring on taking over my job?'

'Which one?'

Earp grinned. He took the two short strides to the bar, gestured for a drink, cocked an eyebrow at Probity. Probity shook his head, moved across to stand with his back to the bar.

'It seems to me,' he said softly, 'that the job you take most seriously is the one that doesn't entail the wearing of a badge.'

'Which shows you're as smart as you ever were, but doesn't answer my question.'

'I'll come back with the same response: which one?'

'What were you doing at Owl Creek?'

'The idea was to ask questions. The way it turned out, I was taking a young lady to her death.' He looked sideways at Earp. 'We were ambushed on the way back. Gunman with a rifle, picked his spot in disused mine workings. I played dead, stayed alive. Sabine Schäfer's lying on her back in the undertaker's parlour.'

Doc Holliday's chuckle was a wet rattle. He spoke without looking up from the solitaire layout.

'Always said you suited black, Wyatt. You're the angel of death. That's two of your girls gone in as many days.'

'What he's supposed to be,' Probity said, 'is a pillar of the establishment, an officer of the law who sees to it killers pay for their crimes.'

Earp was toying with his drink.

'Know what a backlog is, John?'

'What kind of a question is that?'

'Where are we now — September '81. Hell, back in March, a friend of the Clantons and the McLaurys robbed a Kinnear & Company stage over near Ellis — should interest you, because it was carrying silver bullion.'

'Driver was Eli 'Bud' Philpot,' Holliday said, head down. 'Luther King shot him dead.'

'That's right, Luther King. Got arrested, walked in John Behan's jail, walked straight on through and out the back door.' Earp shrugged. 'Never did find the man — '

'Maybe it was him,' Holliday said, 'riding with those done the Sandy Bob robbery.'

'Yeah, I was coming to that.' Earp looked at Probity. 'Doc's talking about yet more friends of the Clantons: Pete Spence and Frank Stillwell. Robbed a Sandy Bob stage over at Bisbee, beginning of the month. We got 'em, but they're out on bail, so, hell, is that another two unlikely ever to pay for their crime?'

'Maybe not. They've been picked up again, by your brother Virgil,' Holliday said, 'this time for the federal offence of mail — '

'Jesus Christ,' Probity said. He pushed away from the bar, swung on Earp. 'You think any of this bullshit is of interest to me? Those two dead girls, one was my sister, the other my sister-in-law — she was Ralf Schäfer's sister, and he's dead too. Surely to God you can see this is all tied in with what's happening at the border, and what's happening there is linked to Owl Creek Mine. If I can see it, I'm damn sure you can too. What I'd like to know is, what are you going to do about it?'

'What do you *want* me to do, John?'

A silence hung over the big room. Holliday had stopped turning the cards. Earp's head was slightly lowered as he looked at Probity with a degree of mockery in his almost black eyes.

Probity took a breath. Smiled ruefully as if accepting some kind of defeat. He spread his hands — then he took a fast step forward, swung a hard fist and knocked Wyatt Earp to the floor.

Holliday uttered a soft, tuneless whistle. His hand had moved. It had covered the shotgun. Now he picked it up with one hand, thumbed back the hammer, let the short muzzle swing casually in Probity's general direction.

Probity looked at him with contempt. He dismissed the emaciated dentist with that single glance, then watched Earp struggle up until he was braced on both elbows. A thin trickle of blood wormed its way from under the downed man's drooping moustache. He touched it with a finger, then looked across at Holliday and shook his head.

'What I suggest you do,' Probity said, his voice harsh, 'is pick yourself up off the floor. After that, why don't you do some real lawman's work for a change, instead of spending your days worrying about Ike Clanton and his boys, and those damned, useless McLaurys?'

And without another word he swung on his heel, turned his back on both men and walked out into the midday sun.

10

'Take my word for it,' Gord Sager said. 'They're both dead, Probity and the Schäfer woman. Saw the bullets hit, plumb centre. They went down like logs, but I stuck it out in the baking heat of that shack to make sure they weren't playing possum. Only movement I saw down that slope was made by the horses.' He grinned, his black eyes wicked. 'Should have brought 'em here with me, shame to leave good horse flesh. Would have added horse thief to my many skills, put money in my pocket.'

It was dusk in Rawton. The big man was sitting behind the late Orin Craig's desk in the jail office. The hanging oil lamp cast its yellow light on him. His sand-coloured Stetson hung on a hook. His hair, face and clothing were still coated in trail dust from the return trip to Tombstone. He was drinking coffee from a tin cup, slouching easily in the swivel chair. His rifle was propped against the desk. There was a strong smell of cordite.

Ellis Quaig was sitting with his legs stretched out, his black jacket swept back. He lifted a hand, fiddled with his string tie, then adjusted his gold-rimmed glasses. He had been staring thoughtfully at the Winchester. Now he lifted his gaze to the new town marshal.

'I should have left it to you to remove the other woman, Annie Schäfer. That way she wouldn't have finished up too close to Owl Creek for comfort.'

'Wouldn't have been raped, either,' Sager said. 'Although, come to think of it — '

'Forget that, what about Court?'

'Yeah.' Sager frowned, absently touched the raw wound on his scalp. 'A mighty cool customer. Tell the truth, I can't make him out. He got back here yesterday, acted as if nothing had happened.'

'Maybe I had him figured wrong.'

'How was that?'

'I suggested to Craig that Court worked for the Pinkertons. I was worried that he'd learned too much from his talks with Ralf Schäfer. But when I think about it, the truth is Schäfer himself knew very little — and now Court seems to be nothing more nor less than a simple town barber who enjoys conversation.'

'Maybe it's safer to trust your first impressions,' Sager said. 'Why take a chance? I looked in on him, he didn't seem worried. If you like I can pull him in for assault on an officer of the law and helping a killer break out of jail. Hell, I surely owe him for that crack on the head.'

'Leave him be. He was in that barber's shop all yesterday, most of today. If he's an agent on a job he's going about it in a very strange way, chewing the fat with old-timers wrapped in a sheet, their chins smothered in soap.'

'Main thing is, you now know when

the next wagon's due to roll.'

'Thanks to you.'

'Yeah, well, it's good having a man you can trust on your side.'

Ellis's mouth twisted as if he found the words of approval distasteful, the suggestion laughable. He dug a cigar out of his pocket and looked at it pensively as he rolled it between his fingers.

'I missed that last consignment,' he said, 'because all I had to go on was a vague whisper one man had heard from a friend of someone he knew who thought possibly — well, you know how it goes.'

'Yeah, but working for a time at Owl Greek gave me the edge,' Sager said. 'I knew who to talk to, the right man to point the way. Or, from Ronan Casey's side of it, maybe that would be the wrong man. Let's say I got it from the horse's mouth, seeing as we're talking in equine terms.'

'Make my day,' Ellis Quaig said. 'Remind me again when it rolls.'

'It's eight o'clock now, twenty four hours until this time tomorrow night, add another six and that's about right. Two in the morning. Same as last time — only tomorrow night we'll be waiting.'

'And you've got the right men for the job?'

'A couple of the Tombstone boys. Ike Clanton. Billy Claiborne. They tell me they're heading for a showdown with the Earps, but they can spare the time to make extra cash. Same goes for me.' Sager grinned. 'Knowing that silver'll soon be on its way into our pockets, as it were, sure beats stealing horses two at a time.'

11

It was dusk when Probity pulled off the trail and approached the Schäfer house. The moon was a huge pale disc hanging above the smudge of purple hills. From that low angle it put the raised arms of the ranks of tall saguaro cacti in stark silhouette. *Like men with their hands hoisted*, Probity thought, *a gun at their backs and them afeard of dying*. And wasn't that a metaphor for the awful happenings of the past couple of days? It was a gloomy thought, made worse by the obvious truth in it, and he could feel his features set grimly as he swung down from his horse.

He wasn't surprised to see, through the front window, the glow of an oil lamp. They had decided, when all three of them rode out the previous day, that the house close to the border was the obvious meeting place. Despite the risk

— for it was possible the Mexicans, knowing nothing of the bloody gun-fight, now considered it to be in their hands — they had agreed to return to it whenever it was convenient to do so. Probity had lingered in Tombstone, so he had fully expected Court to get there ahead of him.

He unsaddled, threw his rig over a rail and let his roan loose in the small corral where it trotted across to Court's mount and the two belonging to the dead Mexicans. Then he walked back across the few yards of open space, pushed open the front door — repaired, he noticed — and entered the big living room. The lingering stink of dried blood had been overpowered, banished, by the appetising aroma of food prepared on the iron stove, and at once Probity realized he was starving.

In the next instant he was shaking his head in disbelief. Ulysses Court was seated at the table close to the window — playing solitaire.

'The last man I saw doing that,'

Probity said, 'had a sawn-off shotgun pointing at my belly.'

'Empty or full?'

Probity stared. 'Would Doc Holliday carry an unloaded shotgun?'

'I was talking about your belly.' Court grinned, and stacked and squared the deck of cards. 'I'm asking if you've eaten, because there's a pan of beef stew still hot out back.'

'I can't remember,' Probity said. He skimmed his hat across the room, watched it hit a chair, then the floor, sat down at the table and said bluntly, 'Sabine Schäfer's dead.'

Court nodded. 'The look on your face, and the fact that you rode here on your own, led me to expect bad news. I'm shocked, deeply, but you look pole-axed and ready to drop. Sit there, my friend. I'll get a steaming bowl of stew, some hot coffee, and you can tell me all about it.'

★ ★ ★

Half an hour was enough time for the story to be told, the stew to be eaten ravenously but barely tasted, and for both men to move across to the easy chairs as darkness settled over the house. There, with cigarettes fired up and tin cups filled from a pot of freshly-brewed coffee, it was Court's turn to tell a story.

'I spent my day-and-a-half in Rawton plying my trade,' he said, 'though nobody was more shocked than me when I was allowed to do so without hindrance.'

'As in you were not arrested?'

'That's it. You were told by Earp that Craig had died, and Gord Sager was wearing the marshal's badge in his place. I had to learn it the hard way. The son-of-a-bitch came and stood in my shop as if his ugly, unshaven presence and the badge prominent on his vest would petrify me. I ignored him. Eventually he sneered, and clumped on out, and I was mightily cheered when the old fellow I was

shaving at the time mumbled something like 'good riddance' under his
breath — although I'm sure his choice
of words was much stronger.'

'So that left you free to do . . . what?'

'Listen.'

'Profitably?'

'Oh yes. For example, I learned that
Ellis Quaig is not an official of any kind
and has only recently taken up
residence in Rawton. The man is from
Tucson, a town he had to leave because
certain individuals in positions of
importance were baying for his blood.
He looks like a businessman, but that's
a façade. Like you see on those shabby
buildings on the streets of any western
town you care to name, it's a false front
he's constructed to hide his true
nature.'

'Risky. Tucson's dangerously close.
How the hell's he getting away with it.'

'A silver tongue. He's the city slicker
taking time out from a busy life to tell
the country boys on the council how to
run their town. I can see them listening

open-mouthed, when all he's doing is passing the time until his plans reach fruition.' Court shook his head. 'And talking of passing the time, he's got himself a good place to do it: before the body's had time to cool, he's moved into Orin Craig's house on the edge of Rawton.'

'Slimy as well as crooked.'

'Sure. We guessed that anyway.'

'But we're still in the dark as to what those plans might be, still don't know what his game is — any more than I know yours.'

The lean man with the piercing blue eyes went still, the coffee cup suspended halfway to his lips.

'Ah. You don't believe I've been entirely honest?'

'If you're a Pinkerton man, I'm Billy the Kid, and we both know Pat Garrett shot him dead at Fort Sumner a couple of months ago.' Probity flicked his cigarette into the empty stone fireplace, absently sipped his drink. 'So tell me, Ulysses Court, what exactly are you?'

'A barber, John, from back east. Nothing more, nothing less. If you want to add something to that description, call me itinerant: I crossed the Mississippi as a much younger man because adventure beckoned, since then I've moved restlessly from place to place.'

'Cutting hair, shaving chins, engaging in conversations. But there's more, isn't there?'

'You hit on it a few moments ago. You asked if my listening was profitable. It invariably is. You see, on my travels I go looking for trouble, and the men who sit in my chair unwittingly feed me information that points me in the right direction.'

'And then?'

'I put away my razor, fold my apron, and set about righting wrongs — although it's entirely possible that from time to time I wrong some rights.' Court smiled. 'Sometimes it's very difficult to tell the difference until it's too damn late.'

'So you're a knight on a white horse,

but with his armour tarnished and dented. And in Rawton, the man who pointed you in the right direction to tilt your lance was Ralf Schäfer.' It was a statement, an acknowledgement of a truth. Probity returned the other man's smile. 'I like that version a whole lot more than that Pinkerton rubbish.'

'So do I. But I'd heard that was what Ellis Quaig suspected, and I took it from there. If that was what people wanted to believe, if that was the word being spread . . . ' He chuckled, clearly amused. Then he fixed his sharp gaze on Probity. 'But that's me, John. Now, what about you? What's your story?'

'Much simpler. The term itinerant fits, but out west they have another name for it.'

'You're a drifter.'

'My parents died young. That was up in the Snake River country. Annie was twenty and strong willed. I was eighteen and green as grass. I didn't know enough to try to talk sense into her, so we went our separate ways. She was feisty, well able to take care of herself. Me, I was lucky enough to hook up with a remarkable man, a big, bearded trapper. He espoused a simple philosophy that's probably not unique, but was new to me, and inspiring. It's guided me from that day to this.'

There was silence for a while. Probity could feel the day's tension draining from his body. The pool of light from the single oil lamp left much of the room in darkness. They were wrapped in an atmosphere rich with the smell of cigarette smoke, of strong, hot coffee — a feeling of . . . of home. Which of course was what the house had been until, in the space of a few weeks, a dream had been destroyed.

'In a way I too went looking for trouble, most often doing it from behind a badge,' Probity continued softly. 'Dodge, Ellsworth, Abilene. I policed them all. But all the while I had the comfort of knowing that somewhere I had someone who cared. In twenty years, we never lost touch. No matter how many miles separated us, we were always there for each other. That's what brought me here — no, that's *who* brought me here: my sister, Annie, but — '

'No buts,' Court said firmly. 'Buts are recriminations, excuses, and what we need to do is put those aside, do some hard thinking and make sure our next move is a good move, the right move.'

'Maxwell Golightly.'

'Who? Is he the trapper you mentioned, the big man with a beard and a philosophy?'

'Plainly stated, by Max, if you leave home with your pants around your ankles, you won't get very far.'

'Why ever not? There's no reason not to, if you can stand the embarrassment.' Court grinned. 'Still, we won't chance it. What we'll do is wait for the next wagon, then follow it, see where it leads — isn't that the plan?'

'Yes. Although, according to Casey there was no wagon. If there was a wagon, he insists it was not from the mines and could not have been carrying silver ore. Which sets me wondering about Ellis Quaig. His actions relating to Annie and me led us to assume that whatever skulduggery he's up to is connected to that one incident here, at the border. But if Casey's telling the truth and there is no silver . . . '

'The demeanour of the Mexican who bled to death, and his dying words, would seem to put the lie to that. And recalling that well-bred, dignified Mex's presence here in this room is a timely reminder that the risk we're taking grows by the hour.'

'Because if there is a wagon, and there's a lantern lit in here when the Mexicans ride across the border to meet it, they'll do so believing their noble compatriot is in residence. They'll ride up as bold as brass, and walk straight in.'

'Catching us,' Court said, 'with our pants around our ankles.'

'So we need to be somewhere else. Far enough away so we won't be seen, close enough to see what's going on. In the dead of night that should be easy. There's that knoll out back, the stand of trees . . . '

'I remember it. Trouble is, it's the only place around here a man could hide, so if they're suspicious, on their guard — '

'They'll be too busy moving that load across the border — whatever the hell it is — and they'll also be edgy, jumping at shadows. If they suspect they're being watched, by Christ knows how many armed men — well, I reckon they'll turn tail and run for it. Come on, let's close this place down and get the horses.'

The moon had floated high above the hills into a cloudless sky. Its light turned the arid land on both sides of the border into a featureless landscape streaked with thin flat shadows, the saguaros looming like makeshift gallows erected by ghostly posses. Probity looked back as they left the house, and in darkness with the door shut and windows like glazed dead eyes the lone building looked forlorn, abandoned.

Ahead of him, Court lifted the pole that let them into the corral, their horses came to them and were quickly saddled. Probity was about to swing up onto the roan when Court raised a warning hand.

'Hear that?'

Probity cocked his head, listened hard.

'A rider. Heading this way.'

'And at a fair lick. We won't reach those trees in time — '

'Then hard in behind the house will have to do.'

'What about the Mex horses?'

'Ragged, underfed ponies. They'll be ignored.'

Jogging, holding the reins high up close to the bits, they led the horses quickly across the open space and into the deep shadows at the back of the house. Glancing back, Probity saw that the horses' hoofs had raised dust even in that short run. In the dry, still air, it hung low over the open ground like a thin mist, taking too long to settle.

With luck that's what he'll take it for, Probity thought: night mist; and then, as the sound of the rider's approach swelled to a staccato drum of hoofs on the hard trail, he was forced to clap a hand over the roan's muzzle as it lifted its head, backed nervously away from the wall.

'Mind the horses,' Probity said softly. 'I'll move further down, come up behind that outhouse. From there I should be able to keep an eye on him without being seen.'

He went around the downhill end of the building, treading carefully, using his ears to follow the rider's progress. He'd recalled that the outhouse had no back wall, an opening serving for a front window. When he stepped inside the crude shelter, his boots crunched on empty tin cans and the sides of packing cases.

He froze, held his breath.

The rider had slowed.

Now catlike in his tread, Probity crossed the six feet of space that took him from the rear opening to the front window. There he stood to one side, back flat against the narrow section of wall, and turned his head to peer out.

It was a couple of hundred yards from the house to the trail. The rider had just reached the point where trail and track joined. That intersection had attracted his attention, caused him to slow, then pull his horse to a halt.

Even from that distance Probity could see him look down, lift his head as his eyes followed the track, then nod in what might have been satisfaction.

Then his heels moved, and at his urging the horse turned onto the track.

'He's coming this way,' Probity said softly. 'You'd better pray those horses stay quiet.'

He had sensed Court come up behind him as silently as an Apache. Now he heard the muffled click of a six-gun cocking and knew the crafty barber had muffled the sound by wrapping the pistol in his bandanna.

Probity smiled his approval, then narrowed his eyes as he focused all his attention on the stranger.

He had reached the halfway point: one hundred yards from the house. Moonlight glinted in his eyes. He had turned his head to look to the right, to the space between house and corral. The hanging dust was almost certainly visible. He seemed to be studying it.

Probity tried to read his mind. What conclusion would he reach? That horses had been ridden towards the house? Was that likely? Probity thought not. Why would any man do that, in the dead of night? No, the most likely cause of the dust was a man riding *away* from the house, the dust petering out because he hit rocky ground as he continued on his way — and in that case raising the dust had been, not carelessness, but a stroke of good fortune.

As if reaching a decision, the man switched his gaze towards the corral, seemed to dismiss the Mexican horses as of no consequence, then looked towards the house. He studied it for what seemed an eternity, but could have been no more than sixty seconds. Then, abruptly, he spun the horse and trotted back to the trail. There he lingered yet again. He kept his back turned to the house, as if it was no longer of any interest. Instead, he looked down the long slope towards the border.

Thirty seconds later, he turned his horse again and spurred hard back up the trail.

Probity stepped back from the window. He touched his brow, felt the film of sweat, felt the salt stinging the recent wound. Court was knotting his bandanna around his neck, slipping his six-gun back into its holster.

'So now we know,' he said.

'Indeed we do,' Probity said. 'Only big man I know wearing a badge and a Stetson of that colour is the new marshal of Rawton, Gord Sager — and if he's showing an interest in the border, it can be for only one reason. He's been sent here, for a reason yet to be determined, by Ellis Quaig.'

12

Probity and Ulysses Court spent a warm night under the stars on the knoll, their horses loose-tethered nearby. They slept easily. They knew that there would be enough noise made by Mexican riders crossing the border, or a heavy wagon trundling down the trail, to awaken them instantly.

Their sleep was made the easier by the strong feeling that there would be no wagon that night. Gord Sager's ride from Rawton to the border was a mite puzzling, certainly surprising, but also reassuring. He had been on his own. From the casual way he had acted they surmised that he had been there to observe. He would go back to Rawton with a clear image of what he had seen committed to memory. If Probity was right, he would report to Ellis Quaig.

Whether they were preparing for

something that would happen tomorrow, or in a week's time, remained to be seen. But, before they spread their blankets, Court had been quietly confident.

'Rest easy, John,' he had said. 'It'll happen, for sure — but not tonight.'

* * *

The next day they moved back into the house. They breakfasted on fried bacon and eggs soon after dawn, then dragged chairs outside to sit drinking coffee and smoking while watching the sun rise. The faint mist that had risen over the nearby Bronca Creek quickly dispersed as the sun rapidly heated the thin, clear desert air.

They'd brought the horses down from the knoll and let them run loose with the others in the small corral. Probity and Court spent the rest of the morning lazing around, drinking coffee, stepping outside every now and then to look intently towards the border, or back up the trail. But it was cooler in the house, so that was where they spent most of their time. Some time after ten Court coaxed Probity into a two-handed poker game played for matches, but he himself was growing restless. Eventually, near midday, he threw down the cards and headed for the door.

'Leaving the horses in full view is too risky,' he said. 'All right, we know what takes place here takes place at night, but most armies send out an advance party, and we can't take that chance.'

'I agree,' Probity said. 'Let's water them and take them back up to the knoll. And this time, the Mex horses go with them. I'm just thankful this house was built near the creek so there's clean water available, for us and the horses.'

'There'd be no shortage anyway. The San Pedro river's less than a mile to the west.'

'Yeah, but I'm talking about water fit to drink without putting a man flat on his back with belly ache or worse. The San Pedro — '

Probity broke off, staring at Court. Then he groaned, and slapped himself on the forehead.

'Jesus Christ,' he said, 'how could I have been so foolish, so blind?'

Court was staring. 'Go ahead, tell me,' he said, 'so I can call you the biggest fool under the sun and we can get on — '

'You don't know much about silver mining, do you?'

'About as much as you could sprinkle on a cigarette paper and leave room for the tobacco.'

'I enjoyed my time with Wyatt Earp,' Probity said, 'so every now and then I've checked the newspapers to see what he's up to. You know he's been a lawman here and there, and ridden shotgun for Wells Fargo, but with his brothers he bought an interest in the First North Extension of the Mountain Maid Mine. Now that interested me, so I read up some on silver mining in Tombstone — and discovered that they've got no water on that plateau.'

'Which makes anything anyone does there mighty thirsty work.'

'Oh, drinking water's no problem. A water shortage means miners dig up the silver ore, but the owners of the mines can't do a damn thing with it. *Processing* the ore requires water — and a lot of it.'

They'd walked across to the corral while Probity was talking. Now they were leaning on the rail, watching the horses without really seeing them.

'I think I know where this is leading,' Court said.

'There are two settlements on the San Pedro,' Probity said, 'some eight miles south-west of Tombstone, which puts them the same distance northwest of Rawton. Charleston's on the west bank, just a couple of dozen crude huts around a post office and saloon. It was put there so the workers in Millville over on the east bank would have somewhere to live.'

'And Millville is where the ore from Tombstone gets processed.'

'You've got it.' Probity was still shaking his head from time to time, but now he couldn't keep still. He began to pace.

'Jesus, Jesus,' he said under his breath — then, again shaking his head, he swung on Court.

'We've been figuring either Ronan Casey's lying through his teeth, or we're on a wild goose chase because what Ralf Schäfer and my sister saw here was a mirage. Or they'd been at the cactus juice, mescal or whatever the hell it's called, or — well, take your pick. But I don't believe any of that, so here's another option: what if Casey was telling the truth when I went there with Sabine?'

'Go on. But keep still, you're making my head spin.'

'He was talking to us about Schäfer. What he said was, and this is near as dammit word for word, '*What he saw at the border that night*' — that's Schäfer — '*was most assuredly not a wagon loaded with silver ore from this or any other of the Tombstone mines'.'*

Probity came to a halt. He stared triumphantly at Court.

'You see what I'm getting at?'

'He was choosing his words, letting you draw the wrong conclusion. What you got from it was that there was no wagon. What he was telling you was that maybe there was a wagon, but it wasn't carrying ore.'

'Over at Millville,' Probity said, 'they mill the ore, reducing it to a fine powder. From that, by a process called smelting, they end up with . . . ?'

'Silver bullion,' Court said. 'And that's what's being taken across the border. Not from Tombstone, but from Millville, which is also closer to Mexico.'

'Christ, I should have worked it out long ago,' Probity said. 'I talked to Annie. She couldn't tell me much, but I let the most important bit of information get swallowed up in the dross. She told me how Ralf had watched the crates being transferred from wagon to wagon. She said he thought he saw just three — and they were not very big.'

'Mm. Couldn't have been ore. And that leads to the realization that we've been foolish. For God's sake, John, silver ore is another name for rock. It wouldn't be packed in crates, it'd be piled loose on the wagon.'

Probity took a deep, shaky breath.

'One of us,' he said, 'needs to pay that town a quick visit.'

Court thumped him on the shoulder.

'You've got the bit between your teeth, you do it. But here's some advice: when you head back, come in the way we did when we rode over from Rawton. When I suggested moving the horses it was because I was getting a real bad feeling. I don't want you anywhere near the house, and I don't want anyone seeing you when you ride in.'

★   ★   ★

'Here,' Court said, 'see for yourself.'

Probity accepted the field-glasses.

They had been on the table in the house, and had probably been used by Ralf Schäfer on the night that sealed his fate. Brass bound and battered, they were also damn near useless, because once the sun went down the lenses couldn't pick up enough light. Nevertheless, what Probity saw through them confirmed what he had spotted as he rode up onto the knoll.

He nodded, returned the glasses, and they moved back from the edge of the trees and sat down on the bone-dry grass close to where the four horses were tethered. Their own were still saddled, because with armed Mexicans just a couple of hundred yards away there was the possibility they might have to move fast.

'So you see, my gut feeling served me well,' Court said. 'They arrived late afternoon, a wagon with two outriders. One of the riders crossed the border, rode up to look at the house. But we'd done well. Moved the horses, and he could see the house was empty. Did some puzzled head scratching, then rode back to his pals.'

'And now, once again, we wait,' Probity said. 'But while we're waiting, we need to figure out how we're going to play this.'

'Before that,' Court said, 'you can tell me how you got on at Millville.'

Probity had been back at the knoll for less than fifteen minutes. His chosen route from Millville had been south along the course of the San Pedro River, which meant he could follow Court's advice and come in from the east. Darkness had already been falling. He stayed in the saddle until he was within half a mile of the Schäfer house. Then he dismounted, removed his Stetson and walked alongside his roan for the rest of the way.

Even from that disadvantageous position, and despite the poor light, he was able to look across his horse and see all the way down the slope to the border. What he saw came as a considerable shock, yet at the same time gave him satisfaction because for the first time he knew for sure they were on the right track. Nevertheless, for the rest of the way he walked in fear of being seen by the Mexicans, because he sure as hell could clearly see their wagon and the smoke from their camp-fire.

'Better than anticipated,' he said, in answer to Court's invitation. 'I went there expecting to learn that Ronan Casey gets the Owl Creek ore processed at one of the Millville plants. What I discovered is that he owns the Tombstone Mill and Mining Company.'

'Dammit, then we're right, he *must* know what's going on,' Court said.

'Why? Far as I can tell he spends his time at the Owl Creek mine. Someone at the Millville plant could be robbing him blind.'

'No.' Court shook his head. 'Think about what he said to you, John, that double talk about no wagon loaded with ore being at the border. Christ, he was laughing up his sleeve, taunting you, challenging you to figure out what he meant.'

'Then tell me this. Why would a man owning a profitable business run boxes of his own silver bullion to the border? Under cover of darkness. Casey made that point, Earp echoed it when I was talking to him in Tombstone. If Casey's selling to the Mexicans, in those circumstances, it's tantamount to smuggling and he's breaking the law and certain to be losing money on the deal — and why would he do that?'

Court's blue eyes flashed in the gloom as he looked thoughtfully towards the border, and the patiently waiting Mexicans.

'Has to be one of two possible reasons,' he said, after some thought. 'Either someone has some kind of hold on him and is forcing his hand. Or . . . hell, I don't know. I was going to say, or it's a matter of life and death — but what the hell does that mean? Can you come up with a situation where, unless he hands over a fortune in silver bullion, someone dies? Maybe that's the hold they've got on him, and the two reasons become one. Or maybe I'm just talking through my hat.'

'It's possible,' Probity said softly, 'that I've come pretty close to the answer already without realising it — or, let's say, without understanding what's there in front of my nose.'

'Try me, see if I can work it out,' Court said. 'Hell, with a name like Ulysses I must be blessed with some intelligence.'

'Sabine, bless her heart, was smarter than both of us put together. It was her spotted it, and since then it's slipped my mind.' He looked across at Court. 'There's a tintype on Ronan Casey's desk. If it's what I think it is — a picture of his wife — then our Irish mine owner is married to a Mexican.'

'Ah, man,' Court said, and he sprang lithely to his feet. 'You know, just listening to that bit of news I've got a story spinning around in my head that gives Casey a clear motive. Remember the Mexican who bled to death in the Schäfer living room? I can see that distinguished feller being a landowner, Casey's wife's father, and fiercely opposed to her marrying an Irishman. I reckon he sent some of his vaqueros up there with their sharp knives, had them drag the girl from the Irishman's loving embrace. Followed that with a message: *Send me mucho bullion, in handy boxes. When I decide I've got enough, maybe I'll return my daughter.*'

Court was watching Probity expectantly.

'What about it?' he said. 'Hell, can't you see it happening exactly like I described it?'

'No,' Probity said. 'It's a pretty theory, but I think you're wrong.'

'Why?'

'Because you're a romantic, and I'm a realist.'

'So what does a realist make of a man with a Mexican wife giving wagon loads of money to her countrymen? If that man we watched die on the floor over

162

there wasn't her father — what the hell was he? If demanding a ransom for his daughter wasn't the hold he had on Casey, what was it?'

'I don't know. But let's say you're right. If the patriarch's death lets Casey off the hook, we're wasting our time waiting for a wagon that's never going to arrive.'

'Gord Sager thinks it is, that's why he was here sniffing around. Mexicans have big families, John. The brothers and sisters, the aunts and uncles, they'll take over from *el caballero*, keep the pressure on.'

'Maybe. But aren't we wasting time juggling theories?'

Court sighed, nodded. 'Yeah, I guess we are,' he said. 'You're not interested in why, you're interested in who. The only reason we're here is because you want the men who murdered your sister and her husband.'

'And the way to them is through Ellis Quaig and Ronan Casey.'

'Right, up to a point; the more we

learn about Casey, the harder it is to see what game Ellis Quaig is playing, where he fits,' Court said. 'But in any event, getting to either of them is going to be tough. The idea is to follow the wagon, but in this desert country we'll have our work cut out. Hell, a rider can be seen — '

He got no further. Probity was up on his feet. The almost inevitable cloudless Arizona skies meant a bright moon, and by its light Probity had caught movement at the border. The three Mexicans were up on their feet, and abandoning the camp-fire. One of them was hastily throwing sand on the flames. Another, the driver, had kicked the team of mules into action. He was up on the wagon seat, bringing it out from under the trees.

The third man had walked forward thirty or so yards and, hands on hips, was gazing up the slope as the swelling rumble of iron wheels on stone-hard ruts announced to everyone listening that a wagon was rolling down the trail.

13

'Well I'll be double damned,' Court said softly. 'There's the proof we need, right before our eyes.'

The wagon's early arrival had caught them by surprise. With the feeling of tension suddenly cranked up several notches they'd covered the fifty yards from the knoll to the Schäfer house at a fast jog, knowing they were taking a chance on being seen, doing their damnedest to keep to the available shadows. Now they were watching, once again from a position inside the tumbledown outhouse.

The wagon rocked past them, squealing and groaning over the trail's deep ruts. It was a flat-bed, drawn by a single mule. The driver was alone on the seat; there was no shotgun guard alongside him for protection from bandits. Lashed on the flat-boards behind him were just two rectangular crates. The words TOMBSTONE MINING Co were stencilled on the visible sides.

'Good that it's there for us to see,' Probity agreed, 'but there never was much doubt. We'd figured out where it was coming from. Now comes the dangerous bit: finding out where it's going.'

The wagon rattled on down the trail, a twisting whorl of dust drifting towards the house in the moonlight so that the two watchers were forced to turn away. They lingered just long enough to see the Mexicans bring their own light wagon to the border to meet the one on the American side, then left the outhouse and made their way back to the knoll. They had checked their weapons earlier. Both men had rifles. Each also had a six-gun and a belt of ammunition. Now, leaving the Mexican horses, they untied their mounts, swung into the saddle and rode carefully through the trees and down the south-western slope that brought them off the knoll.

They rode with infinite care, firmly holding the fresh and excitable horses back to a slow walk. The trail on the far side of the house had its twists and turns, but ran almost due south. The direction Probity and Court were taking put the two wagons, and the men now busy transferring the crates of silver bullion, at an angle away to their left. More trees ran down the edge of the trail all the way to the border — probably surviving on water seeping through the rock from Bronca Creek. They effectively hid Probity and Court from sight.

The intention of the two men to work out some plan of campaign, decide on tactics, had been nipped in the bud by the early arrival of the wagon. That delayed discussion was now opened as they rode through the dappled moonlight, with both men contributing their ten cents' worth.

'The Mex wagon came from the

west,' Court said, keeping his voice down. 'I can't see any reason why they won't go back the same way. If they do, having a wagon when they hit the San Pedro River means they're forced to turn south.'

'Indeed it does, because if I know that river they'd never get the wagon across.' Probity nodded thoughtfully. 'The bullion's early arrival cut you short. You were about to tell me we'd have difficulty following those boys without being seen. I couldn't argue with that. Bright moonlight. Desert country. Sounds impossible, but if we are right . . . '

'I'm sure of it. They'll head down the east bank, and if there's going to be any vegetation higher than a blade of parched grass, it'll be along the river.'

'We could take the horses across,' Probity mused. 'Being on the west bank will put some distance between us and them. We'll be in thick cover on one side of the river, they'll be watching their front with the wagon pushing south out beyond the trees on the other side. If we also hang back a ways . . . '

He drew rein, settled with his hands folded on the horn as he looked away to his left. The sound of men talking came faintly to his ears. Two languages. Difficult to make out what was being said — but so what? They were working men, engaged in a simple task. Straightforward, Probity thought — yet something was making him uneasy. The ghost of Maxwell Golightly was whispering words of warning, telling him something was wrong — and for the life of him Probity couldn't make out what the old trapper was saying.

Court had ridden a little way ahead, then stopped. Now he was watching Probity, perhaps sensing his indecision.

'They're not finished back there,' Probity said, 'so here's another suggestion: let's push on ahead. Riding away from them when they're occupied, getting further away by the minute, is safer than tracking them when they've done loading and got time to look around.'

'What if I'm wrong. What if they head directly south west, across country, leaving us like a couple of wooden Injuns at the San Pedro.'

Probity hesitated. 'You're not wrong. They're using existing trails. And heading up the river is good in many ways — easy on the bones because the ground's softer, they'll be eating less dust . . . '

He knew Court had noticed the slight pause before he answered; knew that the barber was no fool and could sense his disquiet.

'What's bothering you?' Court said.

Probity grimaced, sighed. 'Hell, I wish I knew. Let's just say my bearded mentor of yesteryear is talking to me, but he's got his corn-cob pipe between his teeth and I can't make out the words. Ignoring him, and going by my own instincts — call it a gut feeling — I reckon that before the night is out, something is going to go badly wrong.'

The San Pedro river was a narrow silver ribbon in the moonlight. It flowed north from its Mexican source near Cananea, Sonora, crossed the border, and passed through the settlements of Charleston and Millville on the way across Arizona to its confluence with the Gila River at Winkelman. All along its route it was an unending oasis of green in what was frequently a parched desert landscape. That greenery spread outwards for many hundreds of yards from each bank. Cottonwoods and willows grew thickly, often dwarfed by stands of velvet mesquite.

A clear vision of that lush growth had been in John Probity's mind when he remarked that they would have plenty of cover. He also knew that the San Pedro often ran dry in the summer months. In places the banks were rocky, often precipitous. They had it right: the Mexican wagon would be unable to cross. However, September was too early for the rains, so on horseback he and Court would have no trouble crossing to the west bank. Once there, they could melt into the trees. They would then have some time to wait before the Mexican wagon, weighed down with American silver bullion, reached the river and turned towards the south.

All of this was in his mind, and no doubt being mulled over in silence by Ulysses Court, as they rode out of the east. The ride had taken them less than an hour. The last half mile had been through a shallow arroyo. They emerged abruptly, and were suddenly out in the open. As they approached the river their horses pricked up their ears. The ground beneath their hoofs changed from coarse sand to grass that whispered to them of moisture and, when the fresh smell of the rolling waters reached their nostrils, their pace quickened.

For a hundred yards or so the riders gave them their heads. Then Probity, who was a little way in front, snapped out a warning.

'Look out!'

Not waiting for a reaction from Court he used hands and knees to bring the roan under control. He swung it hard to the right. The swift turn had it snorting in protest. Cursing softly, Probity made for the first of the stands of trees lining the river. He threw caution to the winds and rode hard and fast while trying to do the impossible: make himself invisible, and silence the roan's hoofs.

His heart was pounding. He reached the trees, rode in for a short way and swung out of the saddle. A quick glance over his shoulder as he moved the horse further under the canopy of thick green foliage told him Court had reacted instantly to his shouted warning.

Probity murmured soothingly to the roan, his hand on its neck. Then Court was alongside him. He was out of the saddle, and breathing fast.

'What the hell was all that about?'

'There's a buckboard standing a hundred yards to the south.'

'What?' Court was frowning.

'One man sitting in it. Another standing by, on horseback.'

'Hell fire. Moonlight helps I suppose, but you've got sharp eyes, fast reactions.'

'Sharp enough to see the rider is a big man wearing a Stetson I'd recognize anywhere.'

'Gord Sager?'

'The very same. And if that's Sager, then the man sitting in the buckboard — '

'Has to be Ellis Quaig.'

'Which leaves me puzzled.'

'But changes nothing,' Champion said. 'We still wait for the Mex wagon.'

'Yes, but isn't that what Quaig is doing? Why else would he be here?'

'Sure he's waiting for it. What we don't know is why. So suddenly it's more interesting. When we cross the river and the Mexicans get here we'll be privileged spectators watching a drama unfold.' He seemed amused.

'I think we do know why,' Probity said. 'I think that buckboard makes it obvious.'

'Right. Ronan Casey sends silver bullion to the border where it's handed over to the the Mexicans. They transport it to the San Pedro on the Mex side of the border, and hand it over to Ellis Quaig who takes it home with him. Doesn't make sense.'

'It does,' Probity said, 'if Quaig is giving the Mexicans more than they paid for it.'

'Aren't you forgetting something?'

'Yes.' Probity nodded. 'Casey's Mexican wife. If she's somehow tied up with these cock-eyed transactions, no price would be high enough.'

'Exactly. It's like I said, nothing's changed. And right now we're slipping behind, because the next stage of the plan was to cross the San Pedro.'

'Then let's get on with it,' Probity said, 'and pray that Sager and Quaig keep looking the other way.'

14

Twenty feet down a hard sloping bank of naked earth and tangled roots, the water below them little more than a trickle gurgling between sharp boulders, Court's horse stepped in a hole and went down with a snapped foreleg.

Court fell sideways out of the saddle, rolled most of the way down to the stony river bed. His horse lay still, head down the slope. It's eyes were showing white, it's flanks quivering. It's foreleg was out of the hole, but Probity caught the gleam of the broken bone, the dark shine of blood.

He dismounted awkwardly on the steep bank, took out his six-gun.

Court was scrambling back up the slope.

'They'll hear the shot,' he gasped.

'Can't be helped.'

'I know, dammit.' He was breathless,

saddened. 'You had a bad feeling, and you were right.'

Probity nodded absently. There was a hollow feeling in his stomach. It was always the same, when a good horse had to be put down. He dropped to one knee, drew back the six-gun's hammer, winced as he saw the animal's eyes widen at the sound. He placed the muzzle against the horse's forehead, clenched his teeth — '

Suddenly, from up above, there came the sharp repeated crack of a rifle.

'Now,' Court said flatly.

Probity pulled the trigger.

The horse jerked, died.

Court put a hand on the dead animal's warm neck, rested it there for a moment, then slid his rifle out of its boot.

'I don't know what the hell's going on up there,' he said, climbing to his feet, 'but it came at just the right time.'

He started up the bank. Probity went after him, leading his roan. Gunfire crackled, now coming from two different directions. They ran through the trees until, still under cover, they could see across the moonlit open ground in the direction of the border.

The buckboard had not moved. Ellis Quaig was standing, dark jacket swept back and flaring, hands on hips. Gord Sager was still on his horse but had moved away from the buckboard and was gazing to the south.

'We missed them because we were in a rush, and it didn't occur to us to look further,' Probity said. 'Like us, they were hidden in the trees, waiting for the wagon.'

He was talking about the two men on horseback who were doing the shooting. Though still in the trees they could clearly be seen, and seemed unconcerned by their dangerous exposure. Sitting easy in the saddle they were pouring rifle fire down on the Mexican wagon. It was at a standstill some fifty yards away, the terrified mule backed up in the traces.

'Got here faster than we expected,' Court said, raising his voice as gunfire rattled. 'Must have rolled up soon after us, ran straight into an ambush.'

Yeah, and to do it that way, Probity thought, the gunmen had to be supremely confident, or plumb crazy. Men plan an ambush, they think about cover, surprise, something to rest rifle barrels on so that every shot counts. But sitting there out in the open, their horses so skittish both rifles had to be flapping about like saplings in a breeze . . .

Even as he was mentally deriding the madness of the bushwhackers' tactics, the Mexicans gathered their wits and began returning fire. The two Mexican horsemen were still in the saddle, but were using the wagon as cover. The driver had climbed down from his seat and was crouched by one of the wheels, his rifle poked between the spokes. Muzzle flashes winked red in the moonlight.

'I know those two bushwhackers,' Probity said.

'Yeah, you and your sharp eyes.'

'Ike Clanton, Billy Claiborne. Earp said they're both crazy from birth, and the way they worked that ambush I'd say he's right.' Probity grinned at Court. 'Clanton reminds me of you, are you one of Old Man Clanton's cowboy cattle rustlers — ?'

'One of them's down. The Mexicans got his horse.'

'Makes sense. To save your life, you go for the biggest target,' Probity said. 'And, look at that, if going for the big target doesn't work, well, you get the hell out of there.'

He'd added the last bit in astonishment, because one of the mounted Mexicans had suddenly turned tail and was spurring his horse back along the trail that ran parallel to the border. Whether the act of a man with a yellow streak down his back, or a brave man who knew the game was up, he'd got out just in time.

'Now there's a Mex down,' Court said. 'The bushwhacker who got his horse shot from under him — '

'The moustache says it's Ike Clanton.'

'Yeah, well, he's down behind the dead animal, using it to steady his aim so he can pick them off.' Court said. And then he shook his head and turned away in disgust as the remaining Mexican, the wagon driver, crumpled and lay still.

The shooting stopped. Into the sudden silence Probity said, 'We stood watching that ambush like a couple of kids at the circus. My conscience is telling me we should have stepped in, done something.'

'Maxwell Golightly? Is he your conscience?' Court shook his head. 'He's got it wrong. What could we have done? It was either take sides, and I'd say it was impossible to choose, or get between them. Have you ever tried stopping a couple of drunks in a bar-room brawl? Do that, and you risk getting kicked senseless by both men.'

Probity watched Ellis Quaig drop into his seat. He caught the glint of light on the man's gold glasses. Then, with a flick of the reins, the big man in the dark suit got the horse moving and the buckboard trundled slowly across to the Mexican wagon. Gord Sager was already there, and was off his horse and up on the wagon's flat bed. He was joined by Clanton and Claiborne, who leaped aboard and began dragging one of the small but heavy crates to the tail-gate. The rasp of wood scraping on the wagon's boards carried on the still air. Within minutes both crates of bullion had been transferred to Quaig's buckboard.

'Wondering what to do with the bodies,' Court said softly as the three men jumped down and stood in a bunch. Then, as Quaig's voice reached them, clearly shouting orders, he uttered an exclamation of disgust. 'Yeah, that's what I expected: leave the dead men for the vultures, but take the mule.'

The three men had separated. Quaig swung the buckboard around. Ike Clanton was on foot so he climbed aboard and sat next to Quaig. Sager tied the Mexicans' mule to the buckboard, then he and Claiborne mounted their horses. Led by Quaig, the group moved away from the border. Sager and Claiborne hung back a ways to avoid the dust. Buckboard and riders would pass Probity and Court on their way north — but where were they going?'

'I'm no closer to knowing who ordered my kinfolk's death,' Probity said. 'Quaig's taking a fortune in silver bullion home with him. If possession's nine points of the law, it's his now and he got it without shelling out a single red cent. That means you were only half right. But do we follow, or not??'

'Too risky. I told you Quaig's taken over Orin Craig's house outside Rawton. We know where he'll be, so we can let them go.'

Probity absently watched the buckboard draw level, and said, 'Instinct tells me Ronan Casey is an honourable businessman caught up in a desperate situation that's beyond his control. Ellis Quaig's a crook. My money says he's also a cold-blooded killer. I've a mind to go and talk to Wyatt Earp — '

The crack of a six-gun cut him off in mid-sentence. He and Court had been so intent on the buckboard carrying Ellis Quaig and Clanton they had committed the very offence for which Probity had criticized the bushwhackers. Leaving themselves fatally exposed, they had failed to notice that in trying to escape the plume of dust the two following riders had drifted towards the trees. They had been spotted by Billy Claiborne. Without bothering to shout a warning he had drawn his pistol and commenced shooting.

Even as the crack of that first shot rang out, Court grunted and staggered back against the trunk of a cottonwood.

He was holding his left arm. Blood was trickling between his fingers.

The buckboard drew to a halt. Ike Clanton leaped down, drew his six-gun and began running. Claiborne was charging towards the trees, closely followed by Gord Sager. Both men were snapping shots on the run. Wild shots, but effective. Bark chippings stung Probity's face. A wet stinging told him the old wound had opened.

Without hesitation he slapped his roan's rump and sent it galloping out of the trees and across the open ground towards the abandoned Mexican wagon. Then he drew his six-gun and began returning the fire. With his other hand he grabbed hold of Court's good arm. Backing off, firing, he began pulling the wounded man deeper into the trees.

'Quit shooting, concentrate on running,' Court gasped. 'The more trees between us and them, the more lead they'll waste.'

'Your arm — '

'Hurts like hell but it won't fall off.'

Already, while talking, they had made progress. And Probity knew Court was right. Bullets that had whispered above their heads or clipped bushes too close for comfort began to thump monotonously into tree trunks. The shooting died away. It was replaced by the crackle of undergrowth. Sager had stopped. Clanton and Claiborne began pushing steadily on into the trees.

'We've got the advantage,' Court said.

'Save your breath.'

'They're making so much noise they can't hear us.'

'You're not doing so bad yourself.'

'Far as they know we could be waiting behind the next tree, so they'll move with caution.'

Probity's laugh was a breathless gasp. 'Didn't I tell you those two are crazy?'

The pain of Court's wounded arm was acting as a spur. He was pulling away from Probity. That, in turn, urged

Probity to greater speed. They proceeded in that manner for several minutes. Probity judged that they were cutting through the woods at an angle that was taking them more to the south. Because they were cutting across the woods, it was taking longer to reach the river. The crashing in the undergrowth was fading behind them. He kept throwing glances behind him. In the moonlight filtering through the trees he thought, once, that he detected movement.

Then Court uttered a low warning. They had broken out of the trees into full moonlight. There was a strip of grass and rough scrub thirty yards wide, then the sharp edge of the bank that fell steeply away to the San Pedro's rocky bed.

'Excellent,' Probity said as he joined Court. He stopped, panting, rested leaning forward with his hands braced on his thighs. Some way below, the water was snaking through the rocks. It was a faint whisper of sound.

'Remember Wellington?' he said.

Court grinned. 'Used to hold his forces just over the crest of a hill.'

While answering he had dropped to the grass and wriggled and slid backwards over the edge of the bank. Probity followed suit. They lay flat against the steep slope, below the crest, hats off, six-guns drawn. Invisible.

Probity thumbed shells into his gun.

Court said, 'When we hear them break cover, we poke our heads over the top and blast them to kingdom come.'

They lay there, and listened.

In the breathless stillness the only sound they could hear came from below, the gentle hiss of water against rock. It was like the pulse a man hears whispering in his ears when nervous. But it was a background noise, and of no consequence. Very quickly it was forgotten. The snap of branches told the listeners that their pursuers were upon them.

Probity looked across at Court. Their gazes locked, but unseeingly. Their concentration was on their hearing. They heard a grunt of effort. The harsh breathing of more than one man. The rap of a six-gun against a belt buckle. A soft swish, as of boots through grass.

Court nodded.

With a wild rebel yell Probity poked his head over the edge of the bank and began shooting. Court was slower, hampered by his wound. Then the crack of his six-gun added to the deafening barrage.

Ike Clanton and Billy Claiborne had taken a couple of paces into the moonlight. When Probity and Court popped up out of the earth with guns blazing, they panicked. Claiborne tripped, and fell backwards into the woods. He flapped his arms. His six-gun slammed against a tree and went off. The bullet clipped Clanton's Stetson. He roared, instinctively ducked to the side and slipped to his knees. From that position he got off a couple of shots at Probity. They ricocheted off rock, howled away into

15

'I don't know about you,' Probity said, 'but back there at the river I was aiming high.'

'I was doing the same,' Court said. 'What made you waste good lead?'

'Memories of Tombstone, and Wyatt Earp,' Probity said. 'He told me he's expecting trouble from those two. Our position was unassailable, and I'd have hated to see him disappointed.'

'From what we witnessed, I'd say he'll get his fill of disappointment when he sees the quality of the opposition.'

They were nearing the Schäfer house. Brushing aside feelings of guilt at leaving the dead Mexicans for the scavengers, they had skirted the bodies and the empty wagon and headed east along the southern side of the border. There had been a brief discussion about the lone Mexican who had made the decision to turn his back on the fight and thus saved his life, but the assumption was that he'd have kept running until his horse keeled over from exhaustion.

Riding double on Probity's roan, it had taken them the best part of two hours to get back to the border crossing where the bullion had been transferred from wagon to wagon for the first time. A barren, insignificant location that was yet the focal point of all the troubles, Probity thought, starting with Ralf and Annie Schäfer, and continuing through Sabine's death in ambush to the brutal hail of lead that downed the Mexicans at the San Pedro — a silver crossing now indelibly stained in human blood. Probity was almost overwhelmed by a flood of mixed feelings as he turned the roan up the rutted trail that had been the scene of so much activity.

The house was in darkness, as they had left it, door closed, windows blank. Probity knew that Annie had made sure there was a box of essential medical supplies in the kitchen, and Court was in urgent need of having the ugly, painful flesh wound in his arm cleaned and dressed. The wounded man's bandanna was seeing service as a rough bandage, but it had been clear to Probity on the ride back from the San Pedro that the barber was weakening. Behind Probity on the roan, he had on more than one occasion been forced to cling on desperately as loss of blood brought him to the brink of unconsciousness.

They swung off the trail. The two hundred yards of narrow track to the house was covered swiftly. Probity drew rein close to the door.

'If you're strong enough, I'll put you down here,' Probity said, 'then see to the horse.'

'Go ahead,' Court said, and slid abruptly to the ground.

He stood swaying, one hand tight on the pommel. Probity looked down at him speculatively.

'Was that planned?'

'Let's just say I let go, and the rest happened.' Court grinned weakly. 'Put your horse away. If I can't make it into the house from here I'm not worth saving.'

Probity waited until he had wobbled the few steps to the door, swung it open and stepped inside, then rode across to the corral and slipped from the saddle feeling as bone-weary as Court had looked. The moon was on the wane, the saguaros' shadows pale smudges across earth washed clean of colour, the landscape unearthly. In the faint light, suffering from a feeling of unreality that was entirely new to him, Probity stripped the rig from the horse, threw it over a rail and let the horse into the small enclosure. There was a container of oats in one corner, some hay, a small trough of water. Satisfied that the roan had all it needed, Probity closed the corral.

Briefly, the thought of the Mexican's horses crossed his mind, and he peered across to the bluff. There was movement in the shadows. One or two horses? He hesitated, then turned and walked back to the house.

Court had shut the door behind him. Probity pushed it open, stepped inside, and at once the dormant premonition of disaster awoke and came screaming out of the darkness.

Why darkness? Why no lighted lamp? Why utter silence? Where was Court?

Then, as those thoughts ate up the merest fraction of a second, the door slammed behind him and the cold ring of steel that was all too familiar as the muzzle of a pistol ground into the nape of his neck. A match scraped, flared. A disembodied hand applied the flame to an oil-soaked wick. The lamp's glass chimney was lowered. A brightening pool of light illuminated the room.

'Welcome to the party,' Ronan Casey said from one of the easy chairs. 'You took your time. For a few moments there we thought you'd smelt a rat, and were going to leave your pal to face the music.'

★ ★ ★

The room was crowded, the air thick with the smell of sweat, quivering with an undercurrent of suppressed fury. The ring of steel was rock-steady against Probity's neck. A hand was heavy on his shoulder.

Ulysses Court was pale-faced and hollow-eyed in a chair at the table, sagging limply forward and using the elbow of his good arm for support. Two burly men in rough work clothing were standing near him. The one immediately behind Court's chair was holding a sawn-off shotgun. The other, relaxed and nonchalant at the side of the window, appeared unarmed but had rock-like fists that could fell a steer.

Mine workers, Probity guessed. And deeper into the room, standing with his back to a heavy wooden sideboard, there was a tall lean man in a black suit.

His white shirt was an incongruous flash of brilliance in the gloom. The drooping black moustache gave his face an air of brooding menace.

Wyatt Earp.

His black eyes were fixed unblinkingly on Probity.

'So what d'you reckon, Cézar?' Casey said. 'Are these the men who ambushed you and your *compañeros*, took my silver?'

'*Sí. Por cierto.*'

The man who spoke was the man holding the gun hard against Probity's neck. The words came in a hot exhalation of bad breath laced with garlic.

'I'm an Irishman,' Casey said, 'but even I know that means yes, absolutely, definitely, no mistake.'

His voice rose a notch with each word, and there was a dangerous gleam in his eyes as he looked at Probity. Then he shifted his gaze, gave an almost imperceptible nod. The hand left Probity's shoulder. His six-gun was plucked from its holster. The point of an elbow was driven violently into the middle of his back. A shaft of agony knifed through his lungs. His mouth flopped open in a gasping wheeze. Then the side of a fist, swung with the added weight of a pistol, slammed into the bone behind his ear and sent him stumbling against the table. He fell sideways across it, jarred Court's elbow. The barber slumped, moaned softly between clenched teeth and fell back clutching his arm.

Slowly, struggling to breathe, Probity forced himself upright.

'You're wrong,' he said to the Mexican. He touched a finger to his nose. It came away wet with blood.

The man Casey had called Cézar was grinning. He was unshaven, dressed in a filthy black shirt and flared trousers. One eye was milk-white. His ragged sombrero hung at his back, suspended by a frayed red cord. He held an old pistol in his right hand, Probity's Colt in his left.

'I am correct. *No hay error.*' He waved the old pistol to indicate Probity and Court. 'You were there, and your *amigo*, he was there. His moustache, I recall it. Also, I shoot his horse, he went down, and then' — he shrugged expansively — 'staying there to die did not appeal to me. Besides, I had something to tell my good friend.' He gestured at Casey.

'Cézar is a man I listen to, a man I trust,' Casey said. 'If he says he shot your friend's horse, then that's exactly what happened. Besides, forgive me if I'm wrong, but didn't you boys make it here riding double?'

'Sure we did. Court's horse broke a leg,' Probity said. 'I'm not denying we were there at the San Pedro, but this man is mistaken. We did not take your silver — '

The blow came out of nowhere, and for Probity there was one brilliant blinding flash of red light then everything went black. Time passed — but how long? All he knew was that consciousness returned with blurred vision and a sickening feeling of floating, then awareness of the circle of lamplight and a pair of dusty boots inches from his head.

He was lying on the floor, flat on his back, looking up at the Mexican with the milky eye.

Fighting nausea, he rolled over and struggled to his feet. Cézar backed away, grinning, and Probity knew it was the Mexican's heavy old six-gun that had knocked him off his feet. Blood was drying on his upper lip. Fresh blood was wet on his torn scalp.

A glance told him the mine workers had not moved, but Court was no longer at the table. Across the room, the door to the kitchen was open. A lamp had been lit in that small back room. By its light Probity could see Wyatt Earp busy with knife, basin and bandages, dressing the barber's wounded arm.

A wry smile twisted Probity's lips as he looked at the big, red-headed Irishman. Casey was out of his chair, and had moved to the stone fireplace. He was jumpy, moving restlessly, impatiently. He looked powerful and dangerous. His face was dark with anger.

'You're going about this the wrong way,' Probity said.

'I'm damn sure I don't need a dead man to tell me my business.'

'Is that a threat? The blow to the head, followed by a bullet between the eyes?' Probity shook his head. 'If you kill us, where does that leave you? Exactly where you are now: no silver, no idea where it is.'

Casey said nothing. He dug in a pocket, found a stub of cigar. He looked at it, then grimaced and threw it into the empty fireplace. His face was expressionless when he looked at Probity.

'You've admitted you were at the San Pedro.'

'Yes — '

'Then isn't that enough for me to go digging, to ferret out the truth?'

'This is the truth. We saw a wagon here, we saw wooden crates. If you say they contained silver, then I believe you. Silver *bullion*, not ore — which was the distinction you were making when we last spoke. But it was no longer your silver. It had been willingly passed across the border — that's what we saw. Doesn't it now belong to this man here, to Cézar?'

'It was . . . in Cézar's possession.'

'Are you saying it was not his?'

'It was entrusted to him.'

'Big mistake. Because despite what he says, he has no idea what happened to it. He was ambushed, and he ran for his life — but he ran too soon.'

'So tell me, Probity, if he had stayed a while longer, what would Cézar have seen?'

'He would have seen those crates transferred, yet again, this time to a buckboard that was waiting some way back from the border by the San Pedro river — '

'*Sí.*' Cézar was nodding vigorously. 'I

saw the buckboard, another man, *two* men, your friends — '

'No, not our friends.'

It was Court who uttered the denial as he walked back into the room. His arm was in a crude sling. He had some colour in his gaunt cheeks. His blue eyes were unnaturally bright, but he was reasonably steady on his feet. He said, 'I'll tell you who they were — '

'Wait.'

The snapped order cut him short. Probity held up his hand. He hadn't taken his eyes from the Irish mine owner.

'This is too one-sided, Casey. You're asking questions, demanding answers, but giving nothing away.'

'You're in no position — '

'My position couldn't be better; you're acting tough but my good health is assured because you want something, and I can give it to you. But what do you know, Casey? What can *you* give me?'

The Irishman frowned. 'I don't understand.'

'So try this. Who ordered the killing of Ralf Schäfer and his wife — my sister, Annie? Was that you?'

'Are you joking? Come on, man, it's not in my nature — and, for God's sake, would I do that and tell the killers your sister's body was to be left on my land?'

'Then what about Schäfer's sister, Sabine?'

'You already know the answer to that one, John.' Wyatt Earp spoke softly. He was standing in the kitchen doorway. 'Back in Tombstone I told you Rawton's new marshal, Gord Sager, was looking for you. He asked around, then went after you. He followed you to Owl Creek.'

Probity nodded slowly, realising that at last everything was falling into place.

'If it was Sager ambushed Sabine and me, he was working to orders.' He looked at Casey. 'If you're telling the truth, had nothing to do with any of those killings, then the man who ripped the Schäfer family apart is the man who's now holding those crates of silver bullion.'

'His name?'

Probity smiled. He could feel the change in the room, the easing of the tension. Indeed, the two mine workers had slipped away, one leaving by the front door, the other now in the kitchen rattling all manner of metal implements as he set about brewing coffee.

The unfolding of events over the past half-hour proved to Probity that his instincts had been right, that Casey was an honourable man acting tough because he was caught up in an impossible situation. But while the loss of silver to thieves was a straightforward act of plunder — which the man would surely take in his stride — the reason for the silver's cross-border movements in the dead of night still needed to be explained. It was the motive for murder: an Owl Creek wagon had rolled down to the border, and a young family had been wiped out. Casey was watching him. Probity knew he was waiting for the answer to his question — the name of the thief — but there was also a look in his green eyes that told Probity the man was shrewdly following his train of thought.

'Before I give you his name and where you can find your silver, answer me one more question — and I'll help you by passing on my friend Ulysses Court's fanciful notion. Court suggested to me that the Mexican who died here, in this room, was your wife's father. He believed that she had been taken by her family, and the silver crossing the border was the price you were paying for her return. I think he's wrong, the price way too high to settle a family affair.'

And now it was Casey's turn to smile, but it was a smile that was tinged with sadness. He looked across at Wyatt Earp.

'What d'you reckon, is the man close, or is he not?'

'He's close enough to deserve an answer,' Earp said. 'She was taken, all right,' Casey said, 'but the man killed in this room was not her father, and it's not her family that did the taking.' He paused. 'Her name is Altagracia. She was taken by supporters of Manuel González.'

Court was back at the table. He flashed a glance at Probity. His face was alight with understanding.

'We were discussing that situation, Probity and me,' he said. 'This González, he's been Mexican president since December '80. If your wife has been taken, she must have been working with groups campaigning to put José de la Cruz Porfirio Díaz Mori back in office.'

'González was hand-picked by Díaz when he stepped down,' Casey said. 'There's no doubt Díaz will return, with González stepping aside willingly because he knows what's good for him. But on the streets, that situation is not clear, if it's known at all; on the streets, the Mexican political scene is volatile. Yes, Altagracia was working for Díaz. But now she's in jail. I can't get near her, and those jails are terrible places to be in, especially for a woman — '

'Rat-infested dungeons,' Probity said grimly, quoting Court's words and getting a glare from Casey that was mute testimony to his agony.

'Indeed they are,' he said huskily. 'So doesn't that explain what I'm trying to do, why I'm tormented half to death? The only way I can get my wife out of a hell hole of a prison is by helping to hasten the return of Díaz. The only way I can do that is by providing the Díaz followers with something which I have plenty of, and that is silver.'

'And word of what you're doing reached the ears of men with greed but no scruples,' Ulysses Court said, 'because a man called Gord Sager worked at Owl Creek, and knew men at your Millville plant.'

'A man with muscles but no brains,' Probity said, 'who by this time had moved to Rawton and pinned on a deputy marshal's badge — a step up, maybe, but not one likely to satisfy his yearning for riches. He was just about bursting with all this information he didn't know what to do with, until one day a man in a dark suit rode into Rawton and everything changed.'

'Called in for a shave,' Court said. 'Put his gold-rimmed glasses on the shelf, had his hair trimmed, expressed a liking for pomade. I massaged it into his thin grey hair, but all the time I think he was doing more listening than talking.'

'Likely noticed you had the same habit,' Probity said with a wry smile. 'But it was Sager's responsibility as deputy to notice new arrivals, and in the new man in town he must have seen something that told him his luck had changed. Hell, maybe the two of them got talking over drinks, I really don't know how they got together, and it's not important — '

'So maybe you can quit beating

about the bush,' Ronan Casey said, 'and tell me what is important; tell me what I want to know while I've still got tight hold of my anger.'

'The man we both want is a crook who was forced out of Tucson,' Probity said. 'His name is Ellis Quaig. He's living in Orin Craig's house on the outskirts of Rawton.'

'But he will not stay there for too long now he's got his hands on my silver.' The Irishman came away from the fireplace in a rush. 'Come on, Probity, if we want to catch the man we'll need to ride like the very devil.'

16

It was the hour before dawn, the moon a pale ghost in retreat, the coming day's light a golden promise on the eastern horizon as they set off on the ride to Rawton. They cut across country, John Probity and the big Irishman, Ronan Casey, skirting the knoll behind the house with their mounts at a walk forced by the rough ground, then rejoining the trail and spurring their horses to a long-striding, ground-eating canter. They rode with grim determination, armed with six-guns, and Winchesters in leather boots under their right thighs.

Surely enough armament to take one man who wore his fancy six-gun for show, Probity thought — and at once knew that his thinking was askew.

Wyatt Earp was making his way back to Tombstone with the two mine workers. They were accompanying the Owl Creek wagon, which had been taken far enough up the trail by its driver to be out of sight from the house. The Mexican, Cézar, had crossed the border and was heading home. Ulysses Court was asleep in the Schäfers' house. He had a comfortable room over his barber's shop in Rawton, but was too weak to make the journey home.

The Mexican horses had been brought down from the knoll, fed, and left loose in the corral.

'You hid your horses in those trees on the knoll behind the house so we'd ride in blind to any danger,' Probity said over the rhythmic drumming of hoofs. 'Did you know we'd used that same spot while your silver was being moved?'

Casey grinned across at him. 'Sure I did. For one thing, those Mexican nags gave you away, and then there was Cézar. He's a good man. That one eye of his is as sharp as two of the best. He used to scout for the army, doesn't miss a damn thing.'

'Yet he got it wrong at the San Pedro. He thought he was watching me and Ulysses Court, but the two men doing their damnedest to kill him were Ike Clanton and Billy Claiborne.'

'Earp scoffed at the very idea that those two could be involved.'

'Because they're cowards?' Probity's tone was derisive. 'He's right, of course, but a well planned ambush is the same as shooting a man in the back. It doesn't need courage.'

'So if those cowboys were there, as you say,' Casey said, 'then where are they now?'

'My guess is they're still with Ellis Quaig.'

'Well now, isn't that something,' Casey said. 'And here's you and me thinking of going up against them.'

'The odds are reasonable. Those two plus Quaig and Sager makes it two to one.'

'But isn't the defender always at an

advantage? As an Irishman I well recall the story of Wellington losing many thousands of good men at the Siege of Badajoz.'

'And it's clear to me that you're quoting history to hide your true feelings.'

Casey said nothing, and after that they rode in silence for some time. The terrain was mostly flat, but riven by dry washes and twisting arroyos. Often the trail petered out, the horses slowed by thick scrub bristling with thorns sharp enough to slash flesh. At those times Casey would resort to a rapid stream of Irish oaths, only stopping to draw breath once the trail was regained and the pace picked up.

It wasn't until the low smudges of buildings and the faint lights of Rawton could be seen ahead of them that Casey answered Probity's comment.

'The truth is, I'm scared of getting my hopes up,' he said, as if Probity had spoken only moments ago. 'I'm thinking that maybe this man Quaig will stay put for a while, but then fear hits me because I know that if I was in his shoes I'd be halfway there by now.'

'And if that isn't Irish,' Probity said, 'I'll eat my hat.'

'It is. But, you see, I know he's got my silver, yet for the life of me I cannot work out his next move.'

'What if he hasn't got one? Maybe he planned the ambush, then got a rush of blood to the head.'

'Dazzled by all those riches,' Casey said. 'Sure, but if that's true then there's no telling which way he'll jump, and that makes him dangerous.'

'He's already that,' Probity said, and he was looking ahead somewhat grimly as they rode into Rawton's main street.

He hadn't said anything to Ronan Casey, but only seconds before the Irishman had broken his silence he had distinctly heard the faint, distant rattle of gunfire. Difficult to judge its origin, but if pushed he'd have said it came from a location on the far side of the town.

Ulysses Court had accurately described the late Orin Craig's house.

At that hour the town was pretty well deserted. They rode past the Starlight saloon, took the bend, saw the gunsmith opening his shop and gave him a nod. The only light was glowing in the window of Buck's diner which, for Probity, brought back sad memories of his last meal there with Annie.

Casey cast an amused glance in his direction when they passed the barber's shop, then they were alongside the jail where Probity had spent an uncomfortable few hours, and heading out of town. As the last of the single-storey dwellings fell behind them, Orin Craig's house became clearly visible, down in a hollow, set back fifty yards or so from the trail and draped in wisps of morning mist. It was a two-storey dwelling with a tin roof gone to rust. The picket fence needed a coat of paint. As they drew nearer, Probity saw that an overgrown track led around to a yard with neglected outbuildings at the rear of the house.

'The buckboard could be back there,' Casey said, voicing Probity's thoughts. 'The horses too, for if you're right there should be three of them and I cannot see one.'

'Two. Ike Clanton's horse was downed at the San Pedro, he's riding the buckboard with Quaig.'

'Maybe so, but there are no lights, no signs of life, and already I'm getting a bad feeling.'

'Can you smell what I can smell?'

'That I can. Somebody has been been doing some recent shooting. But I know that already, for didn't we both hear it on the way in?'

He grinned at Probity's look of consternation, then spurred ahead and took the curving track leading to the rear yard. Probity hung back, looking at the front of the house; wondering if, from behind the blank windows, he was being watched by men with guns;

knowing that Casey was right, the birds had flown.

When at last he followed the big Irishman and clattered across the stony yard, Casey was out of the saddle and down on one knee alongside a man who was lying flat on his back. The prone man's head rested in a glistening pool of blood. Casey was feeling for a pulse in his neck. The man's six-gun lay by his outstretched hand. A badge glittered on his chest, and a few yards away a sand coloured Stetson lay in the dust.

'Dead,' Casey said, rising to his feet. 'Shot in the back of the head.'

'Wasn't I saying something about cowards?'

'You were. But why kill Sager? Wasn't he one of them?'

'He'd served his purpose. Now he was just one man too many, and he knew too much.'

'Well, with him dead the odds are moving in our favour. Also, we know the direction Quaig and those cowboys must have taken, for we caught no sight of them on our way from town.'

'They're heading north. And that means trouble. I can't believe I didn't work it out sooner. Quaig needs help getting rid of that silver. He's got Clanton and Claiborne with him, and that gives the game away.'

'Old Man Clanton,' Casey said.

'Right. His ranch is what, five miles to the north of Charleston?'

'It is. And you're right, of course. But if that's where he's going, then the balance has shifted yet again. We must catch him before he gets anywhere near the Clanton ranch or — '

'We'll have Tom and Frank McLaury, Old Man Clanton himself and God knows who else tearing down the trail to join in the fun.'

But Casey was no longer listening. His foot was poking for a stirrup and in an instant he was in the saddle and swinging his horse out of the yard towards the trail. His mind, Probity guessed, was on the two Owl Creek crates, and the terrible fear that if the men from the Clanton ranch reached the buckboard first his silver bullion would be gone for good.

Me, Probity thought, *I want that man Quaig for what he did to the Schäfers.*

Stopping only long enough to rip the deputy marshal's badge from Gord Sager's vest, he swung back into the saddle and set out in pursuit of the big Irishman.

★   ★   ★

As it flowed north from the border, the San Pedro river emerged from the shadows of deep-cut ravines and flowed openly across flatter land. Court, less of a stranger to the area than Probity, realized that this change was of vital importance to Quaig. While the Mexicans had been unable to contemplate a river crossing with their wagon, he knew Quaig would be able to drive the buckboard into Millville and splash across the shallow ford that connected the town to Charleston on the river's western bank.

Indeed, when Probity and Court also took that crossing, they saw fresh wagon ruts in the wet mud that gave them reassurance: they might not be gaining on the buckboard, but they were certainly heading in the right direction.

The early morning sun was a searing golden orb flooding the landscape with light and heat. Still low in cloudless blue skies, it transformed mildly undulating terrain into a land of shadowed crevices. In those hours immediately following the dawn, the San Pedro's waters reflected the sun with such dazzling brightness that a man was forced to shield his eyes.

It was that intensity of light that saved Probity and Court from disaster when, abruptly and unexpectedly, they caught up with their quarry.

The twists in the trail as it followed the river and the land's contours meant that they came riding out of the south-east over the brow of a low hill. The sun was directly behind them. No more than fifty yards ahead, the buckboard had pulled over against a stand of grey-green cottonwoods a little way before a bend in the San Pedro. It was gently canted on the river bank, the three men standing under the trees alongside Claiborne's horse.

If they chanced to look back down the trail in Probity and Casey's direction, Quaig, Clanton and Claiborne would be staring directly into the sun. They would be as good as blind.

Reacting instantly at the sight of the buckboard, Casey pulled off the trail and dropped into an arroyo that began as a gash on the hillside and widened and deepened as it snaked away to the west. Probity was swift to follow. They dismounted, slid rifles from saddle-boots. Both horses wandered towards a patch of grass and began to graze.

'They'll stay,' Probity said.

He scrambled up the rocky side of the arroyo, flipped his hat off and

222

wriggled onto the crest. Casey flopped down beside him, breathing hard.

'If we open up from here,' he said, 'we could drop them where they stand.'

'But it would be cold-blooded murder.'

'And aren't they murderous sons of bitches themselves?'

'They're rough customers, but let's see if we can get what we want without yet more killing.'

'What I want is two crates of silver bullion, and a buckboard to carry it in.'

'And I want Ellis Quaig gazing out at the world through the bars of a cell in the Yuma Penitentiary.'

Casey chewed impatiently at a thumbnail. Like Probity, he was watching the three men at the buck board. They were smoking, drinking from canteens; talking, gesturing towards the crates. They were excited, drunk on success. The sound of their laughter drifted up the slope.

'We don't know how long they've been at a standstill; I can see them moving off very soon now,' Casey said.

'Tell me, how far do you think it is to the Clanton ranch?'

'We forded the river and rode through Charleston, what, maybe twenty minutes ago? Stopped just long enough to get the information we needed, though we were never in any doubt: the town marshal had seen the buckboard, and he'd recognized Clanton and Claiborne.' Probity hesitated. 'The way we've been pushing the horses, I'd say Charleston's two, maybe three miles behind us — and that puts the Clanton ranch no more than a couple of miles up the trail.'

'Well, if you're set against killing them we can at least scare them half to death — though if you're right about the distance, we could be taking a risk. The sound of gunfire carries. It could reach sharp ears if there's anyone out and about, and that would bring the whole crowd down upon us.'

'Or one of those cowboys could make a break for it as soon as the first shot's fired,' Probity said. 'If he reaches the bend in the river, he'll be out of our sight. The two left behind with the buckboard could try to hold us — '

'Which surely tells you that three killing shots putting an end to it at once is the only safe option.'

'Safe, but wrong,' Probity said.

Smoothly he levered a shell into the rifle's breech, pulled the butt into his shoulder, took aim. Casey followed suit, shaking his head.

'All right, so that boy Clanton, there,' Casey said, grinning, 'did you see how he took his hat off his head without moving a muscle?'

But before the Irishman could squeeze the trigger and punch a hole in Ike Clanton's Stetson, the sun, so recently their saviour, now proved their undoing. As they were brought up into the light, the bright reflective steel of the rifle barrels betrayed their position. Dazzling flashes warned Quaig and the two cowboys of danger. Casey got off two fast shots, but Clanton and Claiborne had thrown themselves forward and crawled behind the buckboard. Ellis Quaig, older and slower, tried to leap sideways. He tripped, fell heavily against one of the cottonwoods.

The crack of Casey's shots was followed by yells of anger as splinters flew from the buckboard. Then Probity began firing. He was aiming as close as he could to Quaig without killing the big man. Dust spurted. Stones flew like shrapnel. But Quaig, over the shock of his fall, had wriggled back so that he was in the trees and under cover.

'Stop firing,' Probity said in disgust. 'We're wasting ammunition.'

'What a pair of blundering fools we are,' Casey said. 'If those fellers stay put, we'll need a cannon to shift them.'

'Claiborne's got a rifle,' Probity said, assessing the situation, 'but it's with his horse and he can't get to it.'

'But what about Quaig? He's down, and close to the horse. He can get to that rifle, and if he does he could be dangerous.'

'One man, one rifle — Ike Clanton can't reach his, it's up on the buckboard. We're out of six-gun range, but only if we stay where we are. To get close to them, we'd have to cross open ground. Do that, we're dead men.'

'Ah, but about the open ground now, that's where you're wrong,' Casey said.

He'd been looking about him while Probity was talking. Now he jerked a thumb to their left.

'This dry wash goes in that direction for thirty yards or so, then wanders away to the north. It'd be nice to think it keeps going like that, because it would run parallel to the trail. If one of us was to follow it, he'd be well out of sight and would be outflanking those fellows.'

'I'm younger than you,' Probity said. 'Keep shooting to hold their attention, leave the rest to me.'

He slid backwards in a shower of loose stones, then came to his feet and jogged away down the arroyo.

The regular, spaced crack of Casey's rifle went with Probity as he followed the arroyo's course. It did indeed turn to the north, but always with a slight drift to the West which would take it inexorably away from the trail — and the buckboard was across the trail on the river bank.

Still an easy shot with a rifle — but there were bigger problems.

As it reached flatter ground, the arroyo began to peter out. The rocky walls fell away. What remained was little more than a wide, dry ditch. Probity was exposed. He kept going, but was forced to move awkwardly at a painful half crouch. After twenty yards covered in that manner, he knew further movement was too risky. He dropped to the ground, wormed his way into the long scrub and looked towards the San Pedro.

He was level with the buckboard, perhaps fifty yards away from the trail.

Clanton and Claiborne were still down behind the wagon, hidden from Casey. From Probity's position they were clearly visible. Aware that the angle of the sun meant that this time he would not be given away by dazzling reflections from his rifle barrel, Probity shifted his position to bring his Winchester forward and prepared to fire.

Even as he did so he was startled by the crack of a second rifle, and saw a vivid muzzle flash against the green of the trees. Then he saw Quaig. He had made it to Claiborne's horse, and was down on one knee returning Casey's fire. A swift glance to the right up the long slope told Probity that the man from Tucson was an expert shot. Dirt was spouting on the edge of the arroyo where Casey was hidden, and the Irishman's rifle had fallen silent.

Then, above the crackle of Quaig's rifle as he fired shot after shot at Ronan Casey, Probity heard a wild rebel yell.

There was a crashing in the trees, the snap of breaking undergrowth, and the reason for Quaig's continuous accurate shooting became clear. In that fleeting moment when Probity had been looking the other way, Clanton and Claiborne had scrambled away from the the buckboard and dropped back into the woods. Riding double, they were taking the horse away through the trees, making for the bend in the river — and, unable to get in a telling shot because of the cottonwoods, there was nothing Probity could do to stop them.

Making for Old Man Clanton's ranch, he thought bitterly. Within ten minutes they'd be excitedly spilling their story, painting a vivid picture of a fortune in silver bullion. Armed men summoned by Old Man Clanton would come tumbling out of the bunkhouse, leap onto fast horses, race furiously down the trail. If Probity and Casey were still there at the buckboard, held by the pin-point gunfire of Ellis Quaig . . .

Probity's jaw tightened. He took a deep breath, thought about what was at stake, then savagely dismissed all his noble ideas of right and wrong.

Following the philosophy espoused by trapper Maxwell Golightly which had served him so well for most of his life — think, then act — he slammed the Winchester's butt into his shoulder, settled, and put a single well-aimed shot into Ellis Quaig's cold, cheating heart.

17

Probity leaped up into the driving seat. Casey threw himself down in the back of the buckboard alongside the bloody body of Ellis Quaig. The heavy bullion crates had been manhandled into position so that there was a space between them through which the Irishman could watch their back trail, and fire at any pursuers while being well protected. Their horses were on short lead ropes on either side of the wagon so that they would be out of the line of fire.

It had taken them twenty minutes on horseback to ride from Charleston to where they'd caught up with the buckboard. When they swung it around and set off on the return journey, Probity, driving with fierce determination, estimated that the same distance would now take them longer. But perhaps not by too much. Knowing that it would be pulling a heavy load, when Ellis Quaig hired the buckboard he'd made sure there was a good horse in the traces. And once the horse overcame the wagon's inertia, that weight had its advantages: a fast pace could be kept up for mile after mile with little extra effort; on downhill sections the buckboard picked up speed and the horse struggled to stay ahead.

'I see them,' Casey cried.

They had been rattling down the trail for ten minutes. Probity was appalled.

'How can that be? Riding double, Clanton and Claiborne must still be some distance from the ranch.'

'Yes, but didn't I say there might be fellows out and about? Those two must have come across them halfway, and headed straight back.'

'So — how far?'

'Ah, they're a quarter mile back. So now I'll ask you the same question: how far are we from safety?'

'Five minutes.'

'Then it's done, isn't it. They'll not catch us now.'

But he was wrong.

The fastest of buckboards is no match for a man on horseback. Teeth gritted, hat brim flattened by the wind, Probity urged the lathered horse to even greater speed. The weight gave the wagon some stability, but still it bounced high over ridges, dropped into ruts with a sickening crash that rattled a man's bones. Sometimes it felt as if they were careering sideways as the buckboard rocked off the trail and slid dangerously on the San Pedro's grass banks. But always Probity regained control.

Suddenly his eyes widened, and he smiled grimly. Across the river he could see the tall outlines of the Millville silver plants. They were approaching the outskirts of Charleston.

'Almost there,' Probity cried.

His answer was the sudden rattle of six-gun fire, the deeper crack of Casey's Winchester. A rider came sweeping along the river bank on Probity's left. Grinning, riding with the reckless skill of an Indian, he snapped a shot. Probity felt the wind of its passing, ducked low. Left hand on the taut reins, he drew his pistol. He fired once, over his left arm. The rider howled. His six-gun flew high in the air and he dropped back.

Another rider appeared on Probity's right. He brought his horse up close to the buckboard. Leaning out of the saddle, he clamped a gloved hand on the back of Probity's seat. His teeth were bared. Holding on with that one hand, six-gun held high in the other, he flung himself from his horse. He landed in a crouching position, on two feet, fought for balance. Before he suc- ceeded, Probity delivered a savage backhand blow to the man's face with his six-gun. His grip slackened. He let go of the seat and fell backward into space, teeth shattered, mouth bloody.

But now they were in Charleston, rattling between the houses, the crackle of rifle and pistol fire drawing the frightened glances of early-rising citizens.

Another fifty yards, and Probity swung the buckboard hard to the left and down the slope to the river. Glittering spray rose high in the air as he took it at speed across the Charleston ford, soaking workers heading for the Millville silver plants and drawing angry cries. Those cries were still ringing out when Probity saw, ahead of him, open gates over which a board bore the name of the Tombstone Mill and Mining Company.

As more workers leaped to safety, Probity drove the buckboard in under the sign board and pulled it to a rocking halt in front of an office block.

Startled white faces peered from the windows.

Behind the buckboard there was a sudden, eerie silence.

It was over.

Epilogue

A young deputy was standing outside the jail when John Probity brought the empty buckboard to a halt. The crates of bullion had been offloaded by workers at Ronan Casey's Tombstone Mill and Mining Company. It had been the Irishman's idea to bring the Charleston town marshal across the river to take charge of Ellis Quaig's body.

'It was my bullion the man stole,' he told Probity, 'so he has nothing to account for in Rawton.'

'We'll never know for sure if he was behind the Schäfer killings,' Probity said, 'but who else could it have been?'

Knowing he had to be satisfied with that, he had shaken hands with the big Irishman and headed south to Rawton. Now, climbing the steps to where the young deputy stood watching, he was experiencing a feeling of emptiness. If it was all over — what was there left for him to do?

He got a surprise, and the answer, when the deputy followed him into the jail office.

Ulysses Court was sitting behind the marshal's desk, grey clothes dusty, flat-crowned black hat jauntily tilted, his blue eyes bright.

He grinned at Probity.

'Sorry for taking your chair, but I'm still feeling weak.'

'How'd you get here?'

'I couldn't sleep. Those two Mex horses were still in the corral. I borrowed one.'

'That's not my chair.'

'Oh, but it is.'

Behind Probity, the young deputy coughed. He was no more than seventeen years old. Still too young to get shaved by Ulysses Court.

'Gord Sager's death shocked the mayor,' he said. 'I guess he was panicking, thinking maybe I'd be the new marshal.' He grinned. 'Your friend told him you'd worked as a lawman in Dodge, with Wyatt Earp. As far as the mayor was concerned, that settled matters — if you agree.'

For a moment, there was a heavy silence. Then John Probity shook his head in silent wonder. Think before you act, Maxwell Golightly had advised — but this time somebody else was doing his thinking for him.

'It just so happens,' he said, 'that I have here in my pocket . . . '

And as the young deputy and Ulysses Court watched with obvious approval, Probity took out the badge he had ripped from Gord Sager's body, and pinned it to his shirt.

Author's Note

Many of the named characters in this novel are taken from real life. The incidents in the plot take place one month before the Gunfight at the OK (Old Kindersley) Corral. Across the border Manuel González was the Mexican president, and former president Porfirio Díaz would return to that position in 1884.

Tombstone really was short of water. Silver ore from the mines was taken to Millville for processing, and the workers lived across the San Pedro River in Charleston. Both those locations are now ghost towns.

Those are facts. Deeds done in this story by characters such as Wyatt Earp, Ike Clanton and Billy Claiborne are fiction, and the town of Rawton existed only in the imagination.

We do hope that you have enjoyed reading this large print book.

Did you know that all of our titles are available for purchase?

We publish a wide range of high quality large print books including:
Romances, Mysteries, Classics
General Fiction
Non Fiction and Westerns

Special interest titles available in large print are:
The Little Oxford Dictionary
Music Book, Song Book
Hymn Book, Service Book

Also available from us courtesy of Oxford University Press:
Young Readers' Dictionary
(large print edition)
Young Readers' Thesaurus
(large print edition)

For further information or a free brochure, please contact us at:
Ulverscroft Large Print Books Ltd.,
The Green, Bradgate Road, Anstey,
Leicester, LE7 7FU, England.
Tel: (00 44) **0116 236 4325**
Fax: (00 44) **0116 234 0205**

Other titles in the
Linford Western Library:

APPLEJACK

Emmett Stone

When old-timer Applejack disappears after claiming to have struck it rich, Marshal Rupe Cooley has more important things to take care of, like dealing with the vicious outlaw Cage Drugget. When Applejack is recognized carrying out a bank robbery with Drugget's gang, Cooley saddles up and sets out after them. Meeting more of Drugget's victims along the way, his resolve to bring the gang boss down intensifies. Will he find the hideout in time? And what is the truth about Applejack's fortune?